RED
MOON

RED
MOON

a novel by
Jean Lemieux

translated from the French by
Sheila Fischman

CORMORANT
BOOKS

Published with the assistance of the Canada Council and the Ontario Arts Council. The translator wishes to acknowledge the support of the Canada Council.

Red Moon was originally published in French as *La Lune rouge* by Éditions Québec / Amérique in Montreal in 1991.

WARNING

If you come to the Islands and cross over to Entry Island, if you go past the church and climb to the summit of Big Hill, if you knock at the door of the clinic, you won't meet any of the characters in this novel. Any resemblance to real people or events would be strictly coincidental.

Cover illustration is a detail from an oil on canvas, *Birds and Butterflies among Plants* by Melchior de Hondecoeter, reproduced by courtesy of the Trustees, The National Gallery, London, England.

Cover design by Artcetera Graphics Inc.
Edited by Gena K. Gorrell.
Printed and bound in Canada.

Published by Cormorant Books Inc., RR 1, Dunvegan, Ontario, Canada K0C 1J0.

Canadian Cataloguing in Publication Data
Lemieux, Jean, 1954 -
(Lune rouge. English)
     Red moon : a novel
ISBN 0-920953-65-4
     I. Title.   II. Title: Lune rouge. English.
PS8573 . E5427L8613 1994   C843 ' . 54   C94-900008-6
PQ3919 . 2 . L45L6813 1994

to Jean and Jean

I never go to bed without thinking that perhaps the next day (young as I am) I will no longer be there . . . ; and yet of all those who know me, no one can say that I am despondent or sad in conversation. . . .

Wolfgang Amadeus Mozart

The Clipping

Phyllis Dickson told me the news on the phone. "Thomas, your mother . . . " I had known for a long time that something would happen. I'd done nothing to prevent it.

". . . they found her at the bottom of the cliff."

"Suicide?"

"I don't know. Some strange things are happening. Charlene Collins drowned in the same place yesterday morning."

Charlene Collins. . . . Her face loomed out of the mists of childhood. I hadn't seen her for years. My mother had died this morning. Was there a connection between the two deaths? I stayed cool, irritated almost. I'd have to leave, look after the funeral, the papers, close up the house for the winter. Susan raised herself on one elbow, her belly between us. My irritation was growing, was being transformed into anger. They'd found my mother at the bottom of the cliff. Surely she hadn't killed herself a month before the birth of her first grandson!

"Who did it?"

Phyllis was frightened. I'd shouted.

"Nobody knows. The police are here. They're interrogating everybody. Your mother was there around midnight when your grandmother Eva died. It was the last time anybody saw her."

"My grandmother's dead?"

My grandmother has been living under a death sentence for too long. Her death doesn't touch me. She's been denied the pleasure of knowing about Mother's death.

I flew over this afternoon. Susan is afraid she'll give birth before I come home. As soon as I get to the airport I disappear into a cloud of curiosity. Yes, I am Thomas Patterson, son of the nurse whose body was found at Entry Island this morning. Look at me, I seem perfectly normal. My brother is locked up in Nova Scotia. It's not because of intermarriage, my mother was from England. She came to Entry Island thirty years ago, by way of Saskatoon, and she never left.

A weird destiny. With my camera slung around my neck, I pick up my bag and cut through the crowd, feeling very much the outsider. I hop in a taxi and arrive at the Cap-aux-Meules harbour just in time to get on the boat. Small waves worry the sides of the ferry. They tell me it's been stormy the past few days. On the bridge I see, brought together for these gruesome nuptials, the Pattons from Grosse-Isle and the Collinses from Toronto. The silence is thick enough to cut. The yuppie-faced Collins boys are there. They're ashamed of their mother. Her mascara is running onto her sealskin coat. Too much Florida, madame. Timmy Collins must have found her a pain in the neck towards the end. My aunts and cousins offer me their sympathy. I don't dare to ask if it's for my grandmother or my mother. Robert and I have never been part of the family. We were only tolerated because of Dad.

Off to one side there's a young girl pulling up her collar. She's dragging a suitcase and talking French with the sailor. She must be the nurse who's going to replace my mother. People will miss good old Gladys.

It's been a long time since I've seen the island in November. The fields are yellow and rippling. I walk to the house from the wharf. Randy Aitkens catches up with me in his truck. He looks strange with his two-day beard. I ask him to be quiet and I snap his picture in the November dusk. He invites me to his place. The police have draped phosphorescent bands around the house.

"A few strips of plastic aren't going to keep me out of my own house."

Randy smiles at me. He finally admits that I'm right. He may be smiling, but he's upset too. He's the mayor, after all. Two corpses in his municipality can't be making him happy. It will be good for the tourist trade. They'll put up a billboard: "The cliff where two women died."

"I'm sorry about your mother, Thomas. Despite what people said, we got along well."

Despite what people said. . . . Go to hell, Randy. And the rest of you too. You used to call her "the Old Queen". The Old Queen jumped off the cliff, Randy. Unless one of you pushed her. Or all of you.

"The door's been padlocked," he said. "For the investigation."

You're okay anyway, Randy. We've had some good times. Remember when we stole those boxes from old Sam? You know that I'll go into the house anyway. You're the mayor, you're just doing your job. The wheels are going around in your little head. Who killed those two women? Can you live on this island when a murderer's running around free?

I whisper to him:

"Charlene's death. . . . That must have been hard on you. . . . "

He gives me the same painful look as when I tripped him on his way to the goal, on the ice in the bay.

"Shut up."

His eyes are shining. I ask him some questions. Yesterday morning, the day after Hallowe'en, Borden

Welsh found Charlene Collins at the bottom of Devil's Cape. This morning it was my mother's turn. She died during the night. No leads except for a silver necklace of Charlene's that was found in Mother's kitchen.

"I didn't know Charlene had come back. . . . "

"She's been taking care of her father since the summer. Another thing: the doctor was going around all day in the pants from your father's wedding suit."

"What was he doing here?"

"Stuck on account of the storm. He looked very strange."

I leave Randy. It's almost dark. In the west, an orange frieze sets fire to the ground-floor windows. A new padlock keeps me outside. I take the route of my childhood: the roof over the porch and my bedroom window. Like a thief, I sneak into my mother's deserted house, into the residence grandfather Patterson built at the turn of the century. Luxurious for the time, with a second floor, gables on every side, and Nova Scotia cedar shingles on the walls. Today it's a picturesque little house, barely big enough for two people, that's bombarded by tourists' Instamatics all summer long. The end of the world. When you live at the end of the world, just one step takes you into the void. From Entry, the Earth is flat. Just one gust of wind and it's bye-bye everybody.

Mother was walking along the cliff when a sudden blast of wind from the northwest drove her onto the rocks. When I was a kid I'd put on my heavy sweater and lie down in the wind when it was stormy. Robert would come with me. He was too light, the wind would blow him down. He'd lie in the grass and watch me. I'd hold out my arms and lie down against the wall of air that was assaulting me. The wind would run down my back in a friendly way. And I would fly like that, at an acute angle to the ground, until the wind suddenly changed direction and I fell down. Robert would laugh, choking with the gusts of wind, swallowing the rain that lashed at his cheeks. It must be pleasant, being killed by the wind.

The room is a mess. The bed unmade, clothes and magazines littering the rug. An empty glass on the bedside table, the dresser drawers open, clothes all over. The police have made an unholy mess of everything. Poor guys, it must have upset them. These are the first two murders on the Islands in living memory. For the past few years mother had been slipping. The ground floor was always impeccable, as it was in Dad's day. Upstairs, though, was a shambles. I snap pictures. I want to cry. Why did she leave England? Why did she come and bury herself in this place? Did somebody do her the favour of killing her?

The main floor is awash in the pallid light from the fluorescent fixture in the kitchen. Everything's in order. Dad is smiling under his barometer. And there's the wedding picture: young Bill Patterson, his cheeks flushed from whisky, is celebrating his good fortune. At his side and almost as tall, the dark-eyed beauty, Queen of the Island, the mare from Saskatoon, Gladys Hadfield. Behind them, a cart, one corner of a house, and the clear late August sky.

I'm hungry. I cut my hand, strangely enough, as I'm paring an apple. The house is perfectly still. I sit in the rocker, my hand wrapped in a dish towel. The island lights its fires for the night. What are you good people thinking about? Who among you has trembling hands? Tonight, will you watch television or will you gather in kitchens to untangle the thread of events? The Collins house merges with the dark flank of Big Hill. There's a light in old Timmy Collins' studio. I'll go and talk to him one of these days.

I'm still bleeding. Better call the nurse at the clinic.

Chapter 1
Eine kleine wienie

François Robidoux M.D. took stock of his office. Nothing urgent. His professional conscience, an entity that was rubbery though fairly firm, allowed him to declare that his day was over. Night was closing its eyelid over the horizon. The east wind, which for three days had enveloped the Islands in its hissing sounds, was still throwing heavy seas against the cliffs that bordered the hospital.

François Robidoux was twenty-six years old and looked twenty. Since the departure of his girlfriend, Ginette Beauregard, known as Gigi Bengale, he'd been stirring desires among the island girls. His neatly parted dark brown hair, athlete's body under fashionable clothes, grey eyes, smooth brow, healthy pink cheeks—all corresponded with the image of a boy from a good family, product of the greenhouses of Outremont or of Quebec City's Upper Town. He would have been nondescript if his bourgeois packaging hadn't concealed a remarkable mixture of candour and suspicion, of selfishness and the desire to please.

On his way out he suddenly remembered Jolicoeur's phone call. He hurried over to the community clinic. The corridors were deserted. He found the manager putting in overtime to the melancholy sound of the janitor's broom.

Alain Jolicoeur, forty-something and paunchy, was

a slob with a well-known penchant for poker. On his mother's side he was one-half Havre-aux-Maisons. From that stock came his quick wit, argumentative nature, and a voice that could blast the head off an ox. From his father, a rugged little longshoreman who was concluding a career as pillar of the taverns in Limoilou, he'd inherited everything else, which included a social conscience.

"Ah, François! I'd given up on you!"

As Alain Jolicoeur was both his patient and his team-mate on the JFT Électrique Dinosaurs, François Robidoux enjoyed sitting across the desk from him. Their roles weren't reversed. He had to wait for the not-quite-islander to tell him why he'd been summoned.

Here in the coordinator's office, the universe was divided up, as on the first maps of the world, into two continents: Sickness and Health. On the walls, graphics illustrated the decline of certain health indicators: cigarette and alcohol consumption, unemployment in the 15-25 age group, the percentage of battered women, and so forth. Cards from headquarters showed the penetration of programs of vaccination, sensitization, statistics on cross-country skiing per capita. Even the desk bore traces of this dichotomy: on the left, an apple sporting a seal that testified it had been organically grown, and on the right, sending its fumes into a graveyard of butts, a cigarette. Jolicoeur inhaled steadily, with as much pleasure as embarrassment.

"I'd like to talk to you about a delicate matter. Will you be going to Entry Island soon?"

"As soon as I can get away."

"It's about Mrs. Patterson. . . . "

Jolicoeur dragged on his cigarette, hoping for a reaction from the doctor. François Robidoux said nothing.

"We've had some complaints. She's gone too far this time. It's the mayor who brought it up. A lot of people are saying she's too old to do the job."

"Hard to find someone they'd all agree on."

"We know that. There've been some more serious problems. She chewed out a sixteen-year-old who wanted an abortion. She told the girl's parents. They're furious."

"With their daughter?"

"With Mrs. Patterson. At the clinic we've always had trouble working with her. Ever since she's been attached to us she's looked on us rather. . . . "

"Contemptuously?"

"That's one way of putting it. She finds excuses to skip training sessions. Twenty-five years of service have given her special status. You know her pretty well. Maybe you could sound her out and see what's wrong. She's accumulated lots of leave. She could take a holiday. . . . "

"I get along all right with her. I wouldn't want to turn her against me because of your internal problems."

"External problems," Jolicoeur corrected him, laughing. "We have no control over what Mrs. Patterson does on Entry Island. Can you guarantee that, medically speaking, she's fit to work?"

"I'll see."

François Robidoux M.D. got into his Jetta, pleased with his response to Jolicoeur's proposal. His pleasure was short-lived. Outside the post office he was overcome again by the vague anxiety that had been the main dish on his emotional menu for six weeks now. Word was getting around: Dr. Robidoux was suffering from the pangs of amorous rejection. What a pitiful sight it was to see the handsome young man gulp, hesitate over a drug dosage, or miss an open net in the

Molson Gentlemen's League! People got lost in conjectures as to why on earth Ginette Beauregard would give up such a match.

His mailbox was empty. Even though he was conditioning himself to this daily reminder of his ex's intransigence, François Robidoux felt once more the familiar sting of rejection. Furious at having got his hopes up again, he went to the corner store, picked up a newspaper, left without paying, and drove like a zombie to his house on the Martinique beach, where he realized he'd forgotten to buy milk.

This detail was the final straw. He poured himself a scotch. Sprawled on the sofa fully dressed, he downed it, grimacing, not noticing the dustballs along the walls that bore witness to his increasingly untidy existence. The silence weighed on him. He summoned up the strength to get to his feet and slide Mozart's G Minor Quintet into his CD player.

The violins burst anxiously into the room, taking him back to the September evening when, out of the blue, Gigi Bengale had pierced both him and Wolfgang Amadeus with her poisoned arrows.

The eruption had come with no warning. Arriving home from the hospital late and in a good mood, he'd put on the quintet and turned to the sports pages of the *Journal de Montréal*.

Draped across his plate in a chilly coating of some unidentified sauce, two slices of liver lay accusingly. Across from him, no place had been set. It seemed obvious that either Gigi Bengale had eaten or she'd gone back on one of her diets. She came in and sat down, wearing headphones that exuded the latest recording by U2 from more than a metre away.

Ginette Beauregard, a.k.a. Gigi Bengale, was a young woman of twenty-five, dark and lively and endowed with an awesome critical sense. When François had

met her, she'd been hacking her way through the
jungle of the Montreal media world. On the strength of
what she described first as passion, then as a sex trip,
she'd followed him here to the Islands. Instead of
taking a little break as she'd planned, she had launched
right away into reforming the community radio. She
owed her nickname to certain personality traits and to
her love of tiger balm, which she used abundantly to
treat her migraines in spite of François's skepticism.

Gigi Bengale's relationship with classical music
was a troubled one, based on tolerance. Though François
introduced her to the beauties of the Requiem and the
Ninth, she still maintained that these soporific sounds
were related to other forms of spiritual abasement such
as hockey or TV soaps. The sudden appearance in their
lives of Wolfgang Amadeus, whom François had discovered the year before, had made for a stormy three-
some. At moments of high irritation, when she was
upbraiding François for his oversights or his solitary
tranquillity, Gigi Bengale would call him Amadeus, a
vague but basically affectionate insult that only drove
the young doctor deeper into his narcissism. His love
of Mozart, whose music even accompanied their love-
making, was—along with his Italian briefs, his planned
trip to Asia, his encyclopedia of medical history, and
his membership in the JFT Électrique Dinosaurs—just
one of a group of irritants that she lumped together
under the category of bullshit.

That day, while Robidoux was trying to chew without being noticed, Gigi Bengale, deafened by her
Walkman, loudly declared that Mozart was a pain in
the ass.

"It's pathetic! You're running away from reality,
you're burying yourself in your fucking doctor's world."

François Robidoux had got up and returned
Amadeus to his unmarked grave.

"Explain yourself."

"Explain myself!" mimicked Gigi. "There's nothing to explain. Take a look at yourself, with your businessman's shoes and your designer haircut and your disinfected music! Pum pa pum pa pum pa pum pum pum. . . . "

With her knees raised, Gigi Bengale pranced around the kitchen, trumpeting the beginning of Eine Kleine Nachtmusik. François Robidoux watched her calmly, as if she were a psychotic whose medication needed changing. When they made love, her cheeks took on the same rosy hue just before she came as when they blossomed with anger.

"You got it wrong," he said. "It's pum *pum*, not *pum* pum."

Fatal jibe. Gigi Bengale, standing in the middle of the kitchen, was transformed into a white-hot Vesuvius.

"I suppose you think I'm going to get down on my knees in front of your money and your pathetic little wienie! I'll tell you what you are: you're a bourgeois, macho coward! You live in a bubble! I'm not a decoration. Goodbye!"

Until late that night he tried to extinguish, one by one, the blazes that erupted in the most varied parts of their kingdom. By three a.m. he had gone to sleep, alone, in the big bed, confident that they'd reforest the scorched earth in the morning.

The next day, the *Lucy Maud Montgomery* had transported Gigi Bengale, her Renault 5, her Walkman, and her backpack across the glassy sea. Checking out the house, François Robidoux realized that she'd gone away with practically nothing. She had no possessions, she was free, she was the one who would travel while he stayed behind listening to Mozart and paying off his Jetta and his Italian briefs. That was just one of the considerations that cast him into an existential disarray which was wrongly interpreted as sorrow. Behind a conventional amorous setback stood some more inflammatory questions: Was he, François Robidoux M.D., a mediocre bourgeois? Had he traded his soul for a pay-cheque? Was he now and would he always be too selfish to love someone else? And finally, was it true that he had a small dick?

Freud was barking. Numbed by the scotch and the quintet, Robidoux had forgotten him in his kennel. The Irish setter came in through the porch, soaking wet and dumb. François Robidoux rested his forehead against the animal's salty muzzle and assured him that it was nothing, that things would get better soon.

The phone rang. The hospital operator said that Charlene Collins wanted to talk to him. Would he bring the Mozart recordings he'd mentioned during his last visit?

They exchanged banalities, then he hung up, serene again. At the Coast Guard, the five o'clock forecast announced there would be a faint wind from the south that night. He could cross the next day. He barely had time for supper. At seven, Marie-Claude would be there for their weekly game of Scrabble. At ten, the Dinosaurs would clash with Chez Rosaline's Hot Shots. Though François Robidoux M.D. was in dry-dock, he didn't have time to get bored.

The man holds out his hand. She takes it. At once, the man steps back. She clasps the hand in hers. The man's arm stretches out inordinately while his silhouette shrinks and melts into the night. Now her clammy fingers hold only a dead hand, cut off at the wrist, which crackles when, disgusted, she hurls it to the floor.

Gladys Patterson opened her eyes. In the bedroom she tried to find the seeds of dawn, the grey dots that crept into the depths of the night. Clouds masked the moon. She wanted to sleep some more. She tried quickly to go back to her dream, to find the man again, or his charred dead hand. Her haste wakened her and she thought that sleep would elude her now. With age, you don't sleep so much. She'd said so hundreds of times when old people complained of insomnia. Now it was her turn.

The wind had died down. François would be here today. It was a point of honour for him never to cancel his visits. He would wait for his chance, one or two days, maybe three, then he'd arrive here, impeccably turned out with his doctor's bag, exempt from seasickness and with every hair in place. Dr. François Robidoux could travel around Cape Horn in both directions as long as he had a comb and a change of underwear.

Gladys Patterson smiled. She like Dr. Robidoux, his mixture of candour and cynicism. She turned onto her back. She was gaining weight, especially around her hips. Even though she had sworn that she'd never get fat. She had been slipping for a long time now, nothing could hold her back. She was nearly fifty, and overwhelmed with anguish at the thought of getting old. They could say what they wanted, they would never take those years from her. As for him, he was under her thumb now, reduced to nothing, like her, living on in the baroque parade of days and nights. The world was unhinged, there was no way to stop the mechanism.

Gladys Patterson palpated her belly, her thighs. Night reluctantly returned her bedroom to her, like a pawnbroker. She slipped one finger towards her vulva. She was wet, she must have dreamed. From her basket of fantasies she selected the oldest, the sweetest, the one she'd been using, sad Penelope, since the distant days of her youth, and she knitted a few more rows in the scarf of her love.

Chapter 3
Fifty Knots West-Northwest

At dawn a gentle breeze from the south stirred the fleurs-de-lis on the neighbour's flag. A thin mist hovered above the sea. It felt more like a lull than a sign of good weather. François Robidoux took two CDs, the quintets and the Adagio in B Minor, and drove to the harbour. Between the trawlers, the *Gertrude-Béatrice* was waiting, after three days of idleness, to head out to sea again. On board was a single passenger, a woman who had long ago bid farewell to her thirties, the split ends of her blonde hair fanned out over a shiny new oilskin.

They pulled out of the harbour. The sea bulged under a heavy swell, a legacy of the east winds. Between the choppy water and the unmoving sky, the little ferry glided across the surface of two worlds. The sailor was at the helm. He reached out towards the radio. A voice speaking English came crackling through a jumble of knots and compass points. The sailor turned towards Robidoux and congratulated him.

"Fifty knots west-northwest! Too bad the little nurse has gone back to Cap-aux-Meules. She was more your type than Mrs. Patterson!"

François felt uneasy: he hadn't brought a razor or a change of clothes. How would he look if he had to spend three days in the clinic? And what about Freud? Had he left enough food for the duration?

It was a struggle, but he remained stoical. After more than a year of visiting the clinic it was inevitable that he'd be held captive by the Islands' climate at least once. The adventure was bound to have its share of the picturesque. The Anglos had strange ways of celebrating Hallowe'en. He had heard about practical jokes that straddled the thin line between comedy and revenge, some of which had ended in gunshots.

On their right the dunes of Sandy Hook became sparser until all that floated past was a spike of sand that hurled itself towards the island's dark bosom. Waves swelled beneath the boat, lifted by the breathing of the sea. They were entering the narrow pass that separated the island from the rest of the archipelago. Just then the ruddy-faced captain, keeping to an unvarying ritual, climbed up the stairs from the cabin. Without a word he took over from the sailor at the helm. The latter tossed away his cigarette butt and went to take his turn lying down.

The captain fell into an indolent stupor, barely breaking it to clear an opening for himself in the condensation forming on the portholes. Silently, like a famous extra in a grand production, the *Lucy Maud* sailed past them. The woman's oilskin crackled as she got up to watch it blend into the mist. The captain gave her a surly look. It had been a good month since his last tourist had disembarked, his camera lens fogged over, himself chilled to the bone. What did this one hope to find, between two storms, here on this speck of land that was moving towards winter? He sent a questioning look towards Robidoux, who shrugged.

Entry Island was a vague square of red earth and sandstone pebble, about three kilometres on each side. Its yellowish silhouette gradually filled the horizon. The northern half was embossed with low hills flanked by steep cliffs. To the south, the hills stretched away into a plateau scattered with pastel houses.

The mist frayed as the wind drove off the calm of dawn. Moving automatically, like his superior, the sailor appeared just as they crossed the spit of sand that guarded the entrance to the harbour. He went out on deck to catch some wind. "There's no guarantee we'll be back this afternoon," he noted, observing the captain.

The other man caught a shred of tobacco between his lips and raised his eyebrows. François turned towards the sailor for a translation.

"It depends on the wind," he observed.

He seemed to be enjoying himself. François watched the waves breaking on the pier. The sea was heavier here than in the bay. The breakwater that protected the mooring looked sinister with its fringe of seaweed and its rusty armature.

"Nice place to spend Hallowe'en," murmured François.

The sailor winked at him. The unknown woman started rummaging in her bag. In a tangle of clothes Robidoux caught glimpses of a bottle of hair dye, a water pipe, and a black morocco-bound volume that bore the illuminated title THE HOLY BIBLE.

Chapter 4
The Old Queen

The boat crossed the entrance to the harbour. Almost half the inhabitants were gathered on the wharf, in a happy nonchalance that reminded François Robidoux of the Santa Claus parades of his childhood. Since his last visit, a dozen boats had been hauled into the slipway.

The doctor could make out the tall silhouette of Mrs. Patterson. Prompt as always, she was chatting with the mayor while glaring at the children fooling around on the three-wheeled all-terrain vehicles.

The boat drew alongside. From the faded beams came the smell of fish and gasoline. The unknown woman jumped nimbly onto the dock. Squinting in the wind, she was heading for the road to the church, ignoring the looks that followed her down the wharf.

The doctor cleared himself a path to Mrs. Patterson.

"Hi! How are you!"

Alarmed, François Robidoux sensed that at the last moment the nurse had resisted an urge to kiss him. Quickly, he held out the tonometer she'd asked him to bring. She took it with one veined hand and stuck it in a pocket of her anorak, then ignored it.

"I knew I could count on you," she said.

Her high-pitched voice, filled with subtle inflections, clashed with her stocky build. She still had a hint of the British accent he adored. Without further ado she looked deep into his eyes. In her youth she had been beautiful. Later, wrinkles had hardened her face.

"Have a good trip, Doctor?"

"Did you bring along a pillow?"

The men, with cigarettes hanging from their lips, bent under all kinds of burdens, were teasing the doctor. The dock looked like a battlefield. With inexplicable fervour, the islanders were dragging from the bowels of the ferry the goods needed for their survival. Nails, magazines, rattles, sheets of gyproc, sacks of flour, diapers, TV sets, mailbags, carburettors were passed from hand to hand like precious articles of contraband. Above the show, gulls were wheeling. The captain, his boot on the gunwale, barked the names of the island's three general merchants. Each of them was watching the unloading while a team of brothers-in-law and political backers piled the goods into pickups.

From the *Gertrude-Béatrice* they took an impressive quantity of beer, every case the same brand. The islanders maintained with the breweries short-lived and exclusive relationships which served, better than the years, to mark their past. These cases would swell the reserves that would get them through the winter.

The air was saturated with exclamations and peals of laughter. Once again, they'd outsmarted their Atlantic jailer. They could load their treasures into their trucks and laugh all the way home.

François Robidoux and Mrs. Patterson picked their way through the trucks that were blocking the wharf and set off on her three-wheeler for the clinic. The nurse owned a truck but she preferred the small vehicle, whose instability had terrified her passenger more than once.

The island had an end-of-the-world appearance.

Ramparts of lobster traps were lined up against the grey sky, guarded by truck skeletons and stray dogs. The wildflowers had withered under the autumn winds. Russet hay, a continuation of the rippling waves, shuddered in the bitter wind.

The clinic was a two-storey house that sat atop a low hill. Mismatched carpets on the pine floor gave one the impression of walking on a quilt. A sea smell laden with salt, dampness, and rot seeped into the woodwork. On the ground floor were the doctor's office, a kitchen, dining room, and waiting room. Upstairs, three pastel bedrooms huddled under the sloping roof. It felt a little like being in steerage on a caravel: the floors creaked when you walked on them, the brass beds looked as if they'd shake at the first sign of rolling, the angle beams moaned like shrouds. At every window the sea was bristling with foam.

Mrs. Patterson had prepared tea and brownies. Now she observed the young doctor from the corner of her eye. At the mirror he was brushing off the black sweater that made him look so much like a college student. He was as concerned about his appearance as a young girl. Before leaving the bathroom he would favour himself, on the sly, with the piercing, tender, intelligent, profound gaze that he hoped would come to rest on his patients.

"Who was that woman on the boat?" asked the nurse.

"I couldn't say. Probably a tourist."

"I'll ask Phyllis. She had a hell of a bag for a tourist. I'm glad you crossed today."

They pursued their conversations—to their shared relief—on the neutral terrain of the English "you", avoiding the potential traps of "tu" and "vous".

"Is there a lot to do?"

"Not really. With this weather I wasn't expecting

you till next month. You're going on holidays soon,
aren't you?"

The hospital appointments secretaries kept Mrs.
Patterson up to date about the doctor's agenda.

"I'm going to Portugal."

"With Ginette?"

"No."

"No news?"

"Not a word."

"Miss her?"

"No," he lied.

"She'll come back. A little drink to warm you up?"

He refused. The nurse had taken advantage of the
rigours of last winter to introduce this ritual. It spared
her having to duck into the bathroom before they saw
their patients. After thinking it over, Robidoux had
decided to ignore these habits. She had earned the
right to dull the bite of the beeper she wore at her hip
like an electrode. But while he'd patted himself on the
back for his broad-mindedness, yesterday's conversation with Jolicoeur had left a bitter taste. Should he
have mentioned the nurse's drinking problem? And
why hadn't he done so? Why, in spite of his repug-
nance, did he feel obliged to accomplish this disagree-
able mission?

"You think I drink too much, don't you?"

"No. I told you so the other day."

"I know you think so. You're just like the rest of
them. You don't have the nerve to tell me to my face."
Mrs. Patterson offered these reproaches in an artifi-
cially light tone. For some time now she'd had a
tendency to isolate herself. Her curiosity had lost its
edge and she concentrated on a few subjects which she
kept bringing up and interpreting in a peculiar way.

"If I said that you drink too much, would it change
anything?"

"Maybe."

"You drink too much."

She thought for a moment and took another sip.

"Doesn't work. What am I supposed to do here, besides drink and dream?"

"Why not leave? Your sons are in Nova Scotia. Everybody's looking for nurses."

"What about you? Why are you still on the Islands? What about that residency in internal medicine?"

François Robidoux smiled. Over the months he'd grown attached to Mrs. Patterson. She lived alone in the house that her husband had left her. Her background and her personality had kept her aloof from the community. She went off the island only rarely. Still under the effect of Gigi Bengale's curse, François felt an odd solidarity with her recluse's fate, sensing it was the culmination of his own bachelor's habits.

"All in good time."

They let themselves glide along in the wake of their words. It was strangely dark outside. François had to resist the temptation to switch on the ceiling light. Mrs. Patterson held out the bottle. He refused it again. The opening bars of the Mozart quintet went through his mind with their retinue of queries. Did he really miss Gigi Bengale? His broken heart was only a device.

Changing his mind, he held out his glass. "Just a drop. You seem tired."

"I'm fine."

"If you were my patient I'd recommend a holiday."

"Do you want to take me to Portugal? Did the people at the community clinic ask you to talk to me? Has it got anything to do with that abortion business?"

"No one's said anything about you. You seem tired, that's all. You don't have an easy time of it here."

Mrs. Patterson stood up and angrily cleared the table.

"You want to get rid of me, is that it? I'll have you know that nobody's going to make me leave this island alive! Nobody's going to stop me from saying what I think as long as I can still think!"

François Robidoux shrank back in his chair. The nurse brought out a handkerchief and produced a feeble honk that wasn't able to defuse the situation. There was a silence that was broken by the sound of dishes.

"I'm sorry," said the nurse.

"I shouldn't have brought it up."

Robidoux sipped his drink. Mrs. Patterson busied herself. The hem of her slacks had come down. The cloth hung discreetly onto her shoe, which was outlined with red earth. At university he'd been taught that a doctor must understand everything. Later, he had realized that on occasion he would simply have to wait.

The unknown woman was heading for the church at a good clip, with her nose in the air, when a young man invited her to get in his truck. When he asked, she told him she was here to visit the Reverend Jeffrey Ballantyne.

"You won't find him in the church. Are you a relative?"

"An old acquaintance."

"My name's Randy. I'm the mayor of this island."

With his badly shaved cheeks, his jeans, and his dark glasses, Randy Aitkens looked as much like a pope as a mayor.

"I'm Margie Stone."

"We're more likely to find him at the lighthouse."

The lighthouse stood on the southern tip of the island, circled by a fence freshly painted federal red and white. Since computerization, the keeper's house had been vacant. Now Jeffrey stayed there during his visits to the islanders. He spent most of his time in the lighthouse reading and drinking gin. During his drinking spells no one but Phyllis Dickson was admitted into his refuge. Without grumbling she went every day to clean up this satellite of her rooming house.

The mayor stayed in the truck while Margie Stone, her bag slung over her shoulder, came up against two locked doors. She went around the lighthouse, ran to the cliff, then came back, sniffing the wind. Her cheerfulness was intact.

"He's probably out on a call," said Randy Aitkens. "You didn't pick the best day for visiting the island. There's a storm brewing."

"I'm planning to stay here a while."

"Want me to drop you off at the hotel?"

She thought it over, then accepted. The mayor headed back towards the harbour while his passenger unfurled a stream of praise for the landscape. Another one coming to air her dreams in the countryside. He dropped her off at a house bristling with gables that faced the bay.

"Ask for Phyllis. She'll take care of you."

Randy Aitkens wrapped his words in an irony that Margie Stone, absorbed in the view from the rooming house, didn't deign to notice. She slammed the door and strode away without a word of thanks.

She stepped over a Labrador retriever and knocked. No answer. She went in. An old man abruptly relinquished the TV set. He came up to her, leaving his dentures on the arm of his chair. From the guttural sounds that emerged from his gums, Margie Stone concluded that he was a deaf-mute. Gesturing profusely, the old man picked up her bag, deposited it at the foot of the stairs, then invited her to take a seat on one of the immense sofas in the living room. He replaced his prostheses, grimaced, and left the room, then reappeared with a chubby little woman in her fifties with very black hair.

"I'm terribly sorry," she said, "but the mail just came in."

The old man answered to the name of Winston, the Labrador to Churchill. Phyllis Dickson showed the new arrival to a ravishing room that looked out on the lighthouse.

"Will you be staying here long?"

"I came to visit Father Jeffrey."

The landlady's pleasant face became perplexed. This woman with her hippie airs seemed rather suspect. What did she want with the minister?

"Are you his sister?"

"I'm his wife."

Chapter 6
The Last Crossing

With her back to François Robidoux, Mrs. Patterson finished putting away the dishes. When she turned around her anger had gone.

"Eva isn't well," she said abruptly. "She had chest pain again yesterday. I didn't bother calling you."

"In any case. . . . "

A knock at the door announced the start of the morning clinic. Mrs. Patterson greeted the patients and ushered them into the consulting room. In the beginning she'd looked on the doctor as a necessary evil, barely hiding her contempt for certain fashionable practices. Even if some treatments left him perplexed, Robidoux had been smart enough not to upset the islanders' habits. He'd consulted the nurse about the thousand and one problems no one had talked about in medical school, problems that—more than the syndromes his professors had revelled in—constituted the bulk of his practice. Mrs. Patterson had thought that, despite his pretentious appearance, the young doctor seemed blessed with common sense. She'd been won over when she discovered that he was a believer in the clinical examination.

In college, François Robidoux had devoured biographies of the great nineteenth-century physicians, admiring their powers of observation and their rigour. In the age of the scanner, he decided to develop his clinical sense. Of all the specialties, he had chosen the broadest one, internal medicine. Before starting his residency, he'd taken a professor's advice and left the city. There, away from specialists and sophisticated machines, he had acquired experience.

Trained in the old school, Mrs. Patterson had had to make do for a long time with nothing but her common sense. She'd been delighted to share her knowledge with the future great man, gladly going along with his favourite game, which was guessing his patients' ancestry from their looks.

There was a procession of men, women, and children. They would describe their aches and pains in the same nonchalant way in which they talked about storms and about how hard it was to get supplies. For some, medicine was a novelty and they didn't trust it. For others, coming to the clinic was a pleasant pastime. François Robidoux felt he was being compared with the stethoscope-draped heroes of the TV soaps that the islanders picked up on their satellite dishes.

Just before noon the wind shifted to the west and started gusting. Between patients, Mrs. Patterson made a phone call. Robidoux knew from her voice that she was talking to Phyllis Dickson, her favourite informer.

Mrs. Patterson came back to the office, looking pensive.

"The minute she got here she asked to see the Reverend Jeffrey."

"Who?"

"The woman on the boat."

He'd forgotten all about her.

"She had a Bible in her backpack," he said.

"Maybe she's a nun? Or an ex-nun?"

François Robidoux remembered the water pipe and the hair dye.

"If she's a nun she's in a very strange order."

They had lunch, then they set out on their house calls. He sat behind the nurse, with his black bag under his arm, as they raced down the island's low hills. Mrs. Patterson liked taking shortcuts that would introduce him to new landscapes. In the houses, he picked up conversations with surly old men that had been started last month. Most of them wanted more than anything to be let to die in peace. Others, more anxious, asked for their share of pills. They did so shyly, without compromising the appearance of invulnerability that had kept them alive on this isolated land for eighty-five years. The patients would offer him tea or whisky. Some rounds, notably those in December, called for a strong stomach.

Their first patient was Eva Patton, the nurse's mother-in-law. She was dying of heart disease. The previous spring, after her third coronary, François Robidoux had abandoned any hope of restoring her to a decent life. She'd been given the last rites and the family had made funeral preparations. The next day the eighty-year-old's condition hadn't worsened. She had spent two days suspended in a forest of IV solutions and then, slowly, with no apparent effort, she'd taken a turn for the better. Three weeks later, under the effect of a medical cocktail that kept heart failure at bay, she had boarded the *Gertrude-Béatrice*, swearing to God that she'd never again set foot in an intensive care unit, and that this crossing would be her last.

A tall woman with a leonine head, she looked at things through misty and vigilant eyes. She had to drag herself from her rocker to her bed, breathless after the slightest effort. She had a reputation for fairness, a woman who had raised her children with care. François Robidoux thought she was hanging on for fear of forgetting some detail—a paper to be signed, a card to be sent to a friend, a family problem to be sorted out, a trinket to be left to this one instead of another. This anxiety made her absent-minded and caused her children to say she was reverting to childhood. Patiently and tenderly, they were waiting for her to die. It would happen one day, inevitably, like a poorly maintained motor breaking down.

They found her in her rocking chair, in the care of one of her daughters. The bones of her broad shoulders stood out under her housecoat.

"Hello, Doctor! You finally made it!"

François smiled. She had changed.

"How are you feeling, Mrs. Patton?"

Following hospital practice, he had got in the habit of addressing his female patients by their maiden names. Certain ladies, buried for decades under their husbands' names, smiled to regain their youth in the way that their doctor addressed them.

Insisting that he see her in her bedroom, she rose and, with one hand on her cane and the other on the wainscoting, undertook the journey to her bed. Her feet would tolerate only slippers. The old lady shuffle-kicked along the floor, first one foot, then the other, as if they were cross-country skis. Their muffled gliding seemed to emanate from the pendulum clock nodding in its oak cage. Mrs. Patterson prepared the instruments, then she joined her sister-in-law over a cup of tea.

Eva Patton awaited François Robidoux in her bed, three lace-edged pillows at her back. She asked about his crossing and about the hospital chaplain. She prided herself on never talking about her condition; it was a boring subject. He questioned her, examined her. Her heart was labouring against a surge of secretions that threatened to engulf it from one hour to the next.

"Is that it for today?" the old lady asked.

"You ought to be in the hospital."

She smiled and slowly shook her head. This was their favourite conversation, the doctor trying to convince his patient to go across to the hospital.

"In this weather? Look outside, young man, the boat won't be here for two days."

"You're going to die."

"I certainly hope so."

François Robidoux put away his stethoscope. He was annoyed and he didn't know why. This woman was entitled to die peacefully, at home. He could let her go. She was old, she'd had three coronaries. Her heart was enlarged, tired. It beat absurdly under her thin ribs. He ought to leave her in peace, but he refused to.

"You aren't the one who's going to die," said the old woman, "I am."

The doctor felt his own heart speed up in sympathy with his patient's. His hands started shaking and he felt a knot in his chest. He was suffocating. He picked up his stethoscope and pretended to listen to his patient's chest again. The air came in, went out, amid ominous crepitations. François Robidoux concentrated on breathing slowly, as he'd taught his patients to do.

Eva Patton chuckled.

"Are you asleep, Doctor?"

He straightened up, paler than a ghost.

He trembled as he delivered his verdict: "You've only got a few hours."

"Don't worry. . . . Everything will be fine."

She grasped Robidoux's hand. He'd taken too good care of this old woman. How do people feel before they die? How could she be so calm? The quintet came back to him, along with images of Vienna in the snow.

With her dry lips, Eva Patton sketched a smile. That furrowed face, those prominent cheekbones, had once been those of a lover.

"You've got no regrets?" asked the doctor.

"Regrets! That's for the rich—or for young people like you. The only choice I ever made was my husband. And that was no mistake."

She was still clutching the doctor's hand. He snatched it away. This was a ridiculous situation. What would Mrs. Patterson think if she could see her mother-in-law consoling him?

"Did you take the pills Gladys brought you?" he asked, to disguise his lack of composure.

"I don't take anything Gladys Patterson offers me."

"You aren't very fond of her."

"She killed my son."

"Do you mean they weren't happy together?"

"I mean she killed him! Poison. It's easy to kill somebody when you can get your hands on all kinds of drugs. Such a strong, healthy man! A note from the doctor, a quick burial. . . . "

"There wasn't an autopsy?"

"She showed me a paper. It was all gobbledygook and I didn't understand a word."

While François had sensed that Mrs. Patterson's life with her lobster fisherman hadn't been a perfect love story, there was nothing to suggest she'd actually poisoned him. Did old Eva still have all her wits about her? Was she blinded by the maternal, incestuous love that sometimes emerges from the explosion of memories that comes before death?

He took refuge in a silence that he hoped was understanding. When a patient entrusted him with a disturbing truth, he could bury it under professional secrecy. That saved him from examining it too closely.

"We'll talk about all that tomorrow."

The old lady gave him a look marked with scorn.

"You think I'm crazy, don't you?"

"I have no idea."

"Watch out."

He left her and went to the kitchen to write his prescription. His handwriting was jerky, nervous. He asked for something to drink. Mrs. Patterson was staring at her empty cup, numbed by the bad weather. He doubled the patient's dose of diuretic and told them to call him if necessary.

They continued on their rounds. François Robidoux, perked up by the brandy, looked at the nurse with fresh eyes. Madness? An old lady's imagination? In this country there was a shifting boundary between fable and reality. Even though she'd lived here for twenty-five years, Mrs. Patterson was still an outsider, subject to fears and calumny.

The wind came up again. Certain now that he'd have to spend the night on the island, François Robidoux lingered in every kitchen. He was beginning to understand why these people, despite their harsh existence, often lived to a great age. When the wind came up, when the Demoiselles slipped under the fog, when blizzards danced between the houses, they had nothing to do but wait. Time stopped.

Chapter 7
The Right and the Left

Their last patient of the afternoon was the painter Timothy Collins. An island native, he had lived for a long time in Toronto. His trajectory had been a strange one. Taken prisoner by the Japanese in '41, like many islanders of his generation he'd spent the rest of the war in a forced labour camp. After demobilization, he had worked for two years at various jobs, in Vancouver and Montreal. After that, he had started to paint. It was widely assumed on the island that he'd left in the Far East not only two toes but his mind as well. Paint! Timmy Collins was the clumsiest hell-raiser who'd ever loafed around the wharf at Entry: there was no way he could be trusted with a lobster trap or a paint-brush without his breaking a slat or splattering a port-hole.

On a morning in June five years later, he had disembarked in the company of a dazzling blonde. He called her Inge or Ingrid, depending on his mood, and introduced her as his wife. Later, it was learned that they weren't actually married. They moved into Isaac Welsh's old house, which he bought for three thousand dollars, cash. They came back every summer, soon accompanied by a quartet of children. All day long Timmy covered canvases with violent colours. In September he loaded them carefully onto the ferry. Though the family was poor, they lacked nothing. During the sixties there was talk about an exhibition of his paintings in Toronto, then others in Halifax and Montreal. When his photo appeared in the CPAir in-flight magazine, they had to bow to the evidence: the hell-raising Timmy Collins was one of the ten most popular Canadian painters of his time. After Hong Kong, he'd been right to stay in town spattering canvases rather than come back as a lobster-man at fifty cents a pound.

The gables of his house looked out sleepily at the island. The paint on its shingles was chipped. Without knocking, Mrs. Patterson walked through the swinging door of the porch and into the kitchen. The painter yelled at her to come upstairs.

Since his thrombosis Timmy Collins rarely left the second floor of his house. He lived among his paintings and his music, barely disturbed by the visits of his daughter who carried up his meals and magazines and joined him in exploring the arcana of the tarot. The walls of two bedrooms had been knocked down and he'd fixed up a studio with windows overlooking the church, the lighthouse, the wharf, and all of the Baie de Plaisance from Havre-Aubert to Pointe-Basse. The bare room, where there was rarely more than one painting being worked on, showed few signs of affluence: a sophisticated sound system, a leather chair, a gleaming brass telescope that a Halifax goldsmith had made from his own plans. Timmy Collins used it to observe the boats as they travelled back and forth. The telescope created his only link with the islanders: when anyone wanted to know what was on the horizon, they'd phone old Timmy, who was happy to provide the details.

"Spending the night on the island, Doctor?"

"The boat will never come in weather like this," said François.

"Never."

The painter turned his head and smiled. For a moment he swung into an ancient time when he'd been handsome, ironic, a great seducer. Then he was once again a wheelchair-bound, prematurely grey man.

"How are you getting along, Mr. Collins?" asked the doctor.

"I'm doing fine. Charlene's always going on about my little aches and pains, you must know all about them."

"She called me this week. Said your shoulders were giving you some trouble."

"How about a scotch, François? Gladys, bring me the bottle. It's a day for carousing. Never mind your medicine. Did you bring my records?"

Collins took the two disks and rolled over to his machine. François felt a pang when, of all the tracks available, he chose the first movement of the quintet. The sky grew dark. In the middle of the gasping violins, a heavy rain began to lash at the windows. Twisted in his chair, the painter persisted in manipulating the buttons with his right hand. Although he'd regained some flexibility, he'd had to learn to paint with his left. He would joke that Picasso had had a blue period and a pink one, while he had a right and a left.

His leg was still lifeless. He'd taken refuge on Entry Island and he'd never left. He had lived alone, served by a procession of young girls, sending them packing for ridiculous reasons. Four months earlier his youngest daughter, Charlene, had arrived from Toronto and taken charge of the house. Some of the painter's energy had come back and his left hand showed signs of progress. He talked about it with respectful affection, like a jockey speaking of a stubborn and talented horse. Paintings had started piling up along the walls of the studio again. Despite her father's reluctance, Charlene had arranged to send some to a gallery. Collins feigned indifference, but for two weeks he was incredibly nervous. A phone call brought some peace: his paintings were selling in Toronto, for high prices. A critic had written about a "thematic renewal". His name was being mentioned alongside the most audacious of the young New York painters.

"Goddammit!" he had said, lifting his glass, "if I start painting with my teeth they'll think I'm Gauguin!"

"Isn't it . . . magnificent?" he asked now, referring to the music. "Happy Hallowe'en, Doctor! Gladys, wipe that miserable look off your face and pour yourself another drink. You look like a jack-o'lantern!"

No one but Timmy Collins would dare call Mrs. Patterson a pumpkin. There were some who said the two adored each other, others the very opposite. It seemed to François Robidoux that when the painter came back to the island after his stroke, it had taken him a while to accept the nurse's visits.

Mrs. Patterson poured herself a hefty scotch and knocked back half of it.

"What about those shoulders, Timmy?" she began.

"What do you want me to say? They hurt and that's that!"

"Have you tried the medication?" ventured François.

"Doctor, I've always thought you were an intelligent young fellow. You know as well as I do, those blasted pills do as much good as a kick in the ass."

Timmy Collins enjoyed this verbal sparring. François hadn't won the painter's respect until the first time he'd talked back to him.

"I'm beginning to wonder if a kick in the rear wouldn't be the best treatment in your case."

The door slammed and they heard light footsteps on the stairs.

"CHARLENE!" Collins shouted. "THIS GODDAMN

DOCTOR WANTS TO BOOT ME IN THE REAR!"

"Good for him!"

Charlene Collins might be twenty-eight or twenty-nine. She had a round little face lightly sprinkled with freckles, and mischievous eyes. A mop of tawny hair accentuated her youthful look.

"Hello, Doctor. Spending Hallowe'en with us?"

"I brought my frog costume."

The young woman and her father were taken aback, then they burst out laughing. François Robidoux was proud of his gag. He felt awkward around Charlene. She gazed at him with her impertinent eyes, amused by his candour. The time she'd spent in artistic circles had given her a quick-wittedness he envied. Since Gigi Bengale's departure, he dreaded becoming dull.

"Gladys!" shouted the painter. "Fill up our guest's glass instead of sulking!"

"Charlene's right next to the bottle," said Mrs. Patterson.

François Robidoux hastened to serve himself. The music was screeching now. Timmy Collins rolled over towards the doctor and held out his glass. He pretended not to notice the tension that had settled in since his daughter's arrival.

"My dear François," he began emphatically. "Today is Hallowe'en. Knowing your tastes in art and medicine, I've prepared a game. Do you see these two paintings? Which was done with my right hand, and which with the left? If you don't get it right, bottoms up!"

"Good Lord, Daddy!" sighed Charlene. "How's he supposed to know that?"

"Charlene, this man is my doctor. He knows the depths of my soul, the colour of my shit, the state of my liver, and he almost knows my dreams. He should know my two styles better than some Toronto critic.

After all, I've had a 'thematic renewal'! Ha! Ha!"

At once annoyed and flattered, François Robidoux stood in front of the paintings.

"This one is unquestionably from the left period," he declared.

"Bravo! I expected no less from an intelligent young Catholic. Now it's my turn to . . . how do you folks say it . . . to *prendre un coup*?"

Timmy Collins gulped his scotch. Like all recluses, he gave the impression when he was around people that he was putting on a performance.

"How'd you guess?" he asked.

"Nothing to it. In the spatial organization of the left period, the influence of the non-dominant hemisphere is quite apparent."

"You're a genius. Why didn't you go into police work?"

"Police work or medicine, it's all the same thing: we prevent people from enjoying themselves."

Forgetting the reason for their visit, the nurse and the doctor listened while Collins told Hallowe'en stories. Charlene leaned against a table and giggled in advance at the juiciest passages. The light was fading. With the help of alcohol and the music, François was experiencing a sense of unreality: he was drifting through the North Atlantic fog, surrounded by redheads telling ghost stories.

The laughter died away slowly, and with it the oblivion that had kept them from their usual preoccupations. Mrs. Patterson drained a final glass and opened the doctor's bag.

"You still haven't told us about your shoulders, Timmy."

"To hell with my shoulders and to hell with your pills! Come for lunch tomorrow, François. You can fill out your forms for the hospital."

He spun his chair around and went to put on a new disk. When he lost interest in someone, he turned away with an abruptness that must have won him some enemies.

The visit was over. Charlene walked them to the door.

"Tell me," she whispered to Robidoux. "How did you know the difference between those paintings?"

"The nails holding up the older one were rusty."

"That's what I thought."

She smiled at him. What was the girl doing on this island in the middle of nowhere? Mrs. Patterson was waiting for him in the rain. Charlene offered them a lift in the truck. He declined.

Outside, it was like the end of the world. Gripping the handlebars, her parka billowing in the wind, Mrs. Patterson worked off her bad temper by navigating around the potholes. Far in the east a red moon was rising. When they got to the clinic they were chilled to the bone.

"You can't stay here," said Mrs. Patterson. "You're soaking wet and there's nothing to eat. Come to my house."

François wanted to be alone. He managed to shake off the nurse by promising to come for supper.

The bedrooms were damp and musty. He showered and slipped between sheets of an incredible pink.

His hands and feet were still icy. He hopped over to the thermostat. He could feel his heart pounding and heard again the shuffling of Eva Patton's slippers. For the second time, an anxiety attack had surprised him at the bedside of a dying woman. A month earlier, after a woman patient died, he'd almost lost it in front of the staff.

He had blamed the incident on fatigue. It was true that the patient, a Madame Arseneau, had died under strange circumstances. She was an old woman with a teasing look in her eyes, always joking. After a mild coronary with no complications, she was waiting patiently to be released.

"Imagine a ten-day stay in the hospital for a little palpitation! I'm only doing it to make you happy!"

The day before she was due to be discharged, François Robidoux had found her on her back, arms outstretched and mouth agape. He'd thought it was a joke. "The old crow!"

He'd gone up to her, smiling.

"Madame Arseneau, you shouldn't play tricks like that. . . . You might scare somebody."

Despite his attempts to revive her, it turned out that Madame Arseneau had been steadfastly determined to die. In a daze, Robidoux had stayed in her room. He had seen other deaths. During his internship at the Saint-Luc Hospital, he had tried to resuscitate several patients. In emergency, he'd seen poor devils who drifted on the sidewalks in the less affluent parts of town, or a local *mafioso* with three bullets in his chest. In intensive care, anonymous puppets full of tubes, who for days had barely belonged to the world of the living. For these cases, death was a technicality. He would slip into rooms where nurses and residents were wearily bustling around, taking orders and handing them out. Aware of his place in the hierarchy, he would do something—check arterial gas, do a cardiac massage, an intubation—concentrating on his success. The chaplain would appear. Wedged between respirator and defibrillator, he would drone a few prayers and disappear, a witness from another world. When all hope had been abandoned, the externs would appear, to practise on the cadaver techniques that weren't permitted on the living.

Madame Arseneau's death had shaken François

Robidoux. He'd gone over her file with some col-
leagues. No complaints. Everybody has to die one day.
The same discomfort had taken hold of him again at
Eva Patton's.

Everybody has to die one day. Was he afraid of
death? That was unprofessional for an internist. Should
he search through his childhood? All he could see was
Uncle Roger lying peacefully in his coffin, and the huge
funeral parlour where François and his cousins had
acted up. He remembered a stranger sitting beside the
coffee-maker, who was eventually identified as the
dead man's bridge partner. Uncle Roger had left his
last game with a crash, after returning a club instead of
a heart. The stranger drank cup after cup of coffee,
inconsolable. "But it was true, he shouldn't have returned a club."

François put some Mozart on his Walkman. He saw
again the stranger knocking at Wolfgang's door and
giving him the order for the *Requiem*. The composer
was crippled by debt, forgotten by Vienna, sick. His
music was becoming more and more serene. The approach of death was relieving him of a burden. Strange,
this life that was lent you and then immediately taken
away. God, if He existed, certainly lacked generosity.
So much agitation, only to be crushed like a mayfly on
the windshield of a truck without a driver. François
Robidoux tried to imagine the final moment of lucidity.
The only thing he dreaded was space. Beyond the stars
and the galaxies was that infinity his mind could not
imagine. A fool's game. In the face of these unknowns
all he could do was shudder, like a child listening to a
blizzard in the night, and pull up the covers. Existential. That was the adjective he'd place next to the word
"anguish" in the file of a patient who confessed such a
story to him.

He left a message on Jolicoeur's machine. Would he

feed Freud tomorrow? And take him out to get some exercise? He didn't know when he'd be back. Poor Freud.

The music moved into a major key. François Robidoux's heart slowed down. The wind was whistling in the cornice of the house. The ceiling was spinning and reminding him of Timmy Collins's stories. In ten minutes he was asleep.

Chapter 8
The Lighthouse-Keeper

Winston bent over to light the stove. An hour earlier he'd turned off the thermostats to indulge for the first time that autumn his passion for wood fires. Phyllis Dickson glared at him. He ignored her. That woman upstairs was bothering her. He hadn't grasped what they'd been telling each other during supper. Phyllis didn't seem overly fond of her.

In fact the unknown woman was on her way downstairs now, flamboyant in her tourist's oilskin. With her bag under her arm she was setting out on an expedition —at eight p.m., with the threat of high winds. Phyllis asked where she was going. On the woman's lips, Winston read the name Jeffrey. Phyllis scowled and turned her head. The woman left, unconcerned about her reaction, a smile clinging to her puffy face.

Margie Stone started walking towards the lighthouse. Its beam had just been superimposed over the moonlight, illuminating here and there a stunted spruce, a shed, the skeleton of a truck.

The lighthouse keeper's house was shut. Margie Stone knocked at the door.

"Jeffrey! I know you're there. Open up, honey. . . . "

No reply. Margie Stone put down her bag and sat at the foot of the door, getting up from time to time to knock gently.

Half an hour later she heard the bolt slide. She

picked up her bag and walked into a low room that smelled of alcohol.

Father Jeffrey Ballantyne, his back conspicuously turned, was frying eggs.

"Are you hungry?"

"I ate at Mrs. Dickson's. Oh, Jeffrey!"

She rushed over to embrace him. The minister was a dark, sickly-looking, unkempt man with trembling hands. He turned around to put the blazing stove between the woman and himself. Clinging to his shield, he manoeuvred his way to the table.

"What are you doing here? You promised me. . . . "

"I'm out of there. I left everything in Sydney."

Without looking at her, the priest sat down to eat.

"I'm free," whispered Margie Stone.

The adjective hung in the air like a password. The priest laughed convulsively.

"FREE! Mrs. Fletcher is FREE!"

"Why are you calling me Mrs. Fletcher?"

"Mrs. Fletcher, a married woman with three children, is free! Take a look at yourself! You look like a boiled apple."

As he was losing his composure, Margie Stone regained hers. Her face was stamped with benevolence as she gained control of the situation.

"It was bound to happen, Jeffrey. We were destined to get back together. Don't worry, everything will be like it was before."

"I told you not to come here any more."

"You're in love with me."

"Leave me alone."

"You're in love with me. These things happen. If we lived together for a while everything would get straightened out."

"Live together! You can't leave your children. Go away."

"They're old enough to take care of themselves. I've got a present for you."

She took the Bible from her bag and held it out to him. He peered at the book wearily and then, cautiously holding it between thumb and forefinger, dumped it in the garbage. He came back and sat down, took a deep breath, and sent his plate flying against the refrigerator.

"Good for you," said Margie Stone.

"Go back to Phyllis Dickson's and get on the first ferry."

"I'm staying."

"I'm going."

"You'll come back and I'll be waiting for you."

Exasperated, Jeffrey Ballantyne went to take refuge in the next room. Margie Stone turned off the stove, pulled the curtains, and undressed, then appeared, naked, in the living room. She put on some music, sat on the minister's lap, and began to draw him from his torpor. He fidgeted on the sofa, moaned, cried. In a sudden burst of energy he grabbed her arm and threw her out, bag and baggage, threatening to kill her if she started up again.

With chattering teeth, Margie Stone scooped up her flashy duds. Once she was dressed, she calmed down. She went to the door.

"See you tomorrow, Jeffrey! I love you."

The priest watched her walk away. The pain in his stomach returned. He knocked back some gin, imagining himself hemorrhaging, vomiting rivers of blood, being rushed to hospital by respectfully grieving parishioners.

He went outside and headed in the direction of the cliffs. Waves pounded at the island's flanks. Pebbles snickered along the beach. He walked beside the silvery seething water, then went back to the lighthouse.

Jeffrey salvaged the Bible from the garbage can and cleaned it off. The light in his bedroom window was on until late that night.

Chapter 9
Mascara on the Oboe

The phone wrenched François Robidoux from a dream-less sleep. It was pitch-dark. The rain was still falling, not so violently now. In a mellow voice, Mrs. Patterson announced that the lamb was in the process of burning to a crisp.

He pulled on his wet clothes. Numb with cold, hunger and alcohol gnawing at his stomach, he walked to the nurse's house. She lived a hundred metres from the clinic, on the road that led to the cliffs. Stars were appearing behind Havre-Aubert. The rain shivered under contrary winds.

Bill Patterson's '69 Ford truck was dozing next to the nurse's house. On this island where vehicles succumbed at an early age, victims of roads filled with ruts, its survival was almost miraculous. His widow used it only rarely, to safeguard a vestige of her past.

Mrs. Patterson had changed into a dress and had outlined her big eyes in black. The dining-room table was set for two. On the walls and the TV set, nautical photos and objects evoked her husband's memory. A country singer's cavernous voice poured from a tape deck. The lighthouse beam struck a languid beat against the silver utensils.

"You're soaking wet. Here, put on these dry clothes. I'll wash yours."

In the bathroom François discovered, carefully

folded, the mothballed components of what from all appearances had been the late Bill Patterson's wedding suit.

"You really want me to put that on?"

"It's all I've got. Do you want my bathrobe?"

"No thanks."

François decided to play along. He dressed carefully, down to the cufflinks and bowtie. The only things missing were shoes and a hat. He gazed at himself in the mirror: he looked like a wedding usher who'd been up all night playing cards.

He made his entrance into the kitchen. Mrs. Patterson was waiting for him with a top hat in one hand and a glass of wine in the other.

"Sorry. I gave Bill's brother the shoes. You look very elegant."

She adjusted his collar, his bowtie, and his hat. She was drunk.

Children in Hallowe'en costumes started ringing the bell at the soup and didn't stop till dessert. They came in and froze at the sight of the undertaker who was eating supper with Mrs. Patterson. Sometimes there was an adult with them, who didn't fail to compliment Robidoux on his get-up.

While the lamb was excellent, the Riesling didn't go with it at all. Mrs. Patterson was drinking heavily and made sure that François's glass was always full. Despite the wedding suit, the doctor felt comfortable with this woman who hadn't shared a cosy dinner with a man for ages. He discovered he had an unfamiliar wit. His hostess smiled, twirling her wineglass in her midwife's hand. She put on a Tchaikovsky symphony, whose soaring phrases impressed the monsters who came through the porch. Then the dinner-table atmosphere changed and Mrs. Patterson grew distant, nebulous. François Robidoux's phrases were lost amid the disorder of the table.

She was listening to the music.

"Do you like Tchaikovsky?" (He was proud that he'd recognized the composer.)

"He was my father's favourite composer. He used to play that theme at night to soothe me."

"He played the flute?"

"Oboe," she corrected him condescendingly. "My father was oboist with the London Philharmonic. He was a handsome man, happy-go-lucky and childlike. He gave up the piano for the oboe. No one could understand why. He was glad to give the A and play his little solos. He was incredibly unambitious."

François sipped his wine. He suddenly felt very young.

"How did he wind up in Saskatoon?"

"My mother died in a bombing raid. With my brother Jimmy."

"I'm sorry."

"Nothing to be sorry about. It was all so long ago. Sometimes I wonder if it was just a bad movie."

Now François Robidoux felt uncomfortable. His work kept him in daily contact with pain. For him, emotion was accompanied, like the work of an aching muscle, by a grimace of the soul.

"That must have been very hard on you. . . . "

"I was five years old. Father and I moved into a little apartment. He left the orchestra to look after me. He'd spend hours telling me stories, playing, taking me to the zoo. He'd check on me at night to see if I was cold, if I was breathing properly, if I was dead. I'd go to bed before him. It reassured him.

"Then we started running out of money. He had to go back to the piano, playing the tango in nightclubs. He left me with a neighbour, a kindly drunk who'd fall asleep listening to the BBC. Eventually, he realized it would be simpler to leave me by myself.

"When I was eight he took me to see my first western. It was an inspiration: I wanted to go to America. So then, in the same way that he used to take me to the park and the zoo and the movies, he took me to America. He chose Canada because of the Indians. My father thought Canadian Indians were more genuine than American ones.

"We visited Paris, Rome, Vienna. He was anxious to show me Europe before we went to the New World. In Amsterdam we boarded a freighter that was full of emigrants from Central Europe. On the boat he met a German woman named Maria. Her husband had died at the front. She had a son my age, Hans, who played the piano. They spent time together. Three months later, we left Halifax to join them in Saskatoon."

The music had stopped. Mrs. Patterson was too caught up in her story to notice.

"And then?"

"They didn't have children. I don't think they wanted any. They had their hands full with Hans and me. We'd stopped getting along on the day of the wedding. I was jealous over my father, I suppose. He gave Hans music lessons and praised his talent. I thought he cheated. He played the piano like a trained monkey. I was right: today, he's an accountant. He's fantastic at mental arithmetic. He bets at the bar with his friends.

"My father opened a music store. He played the oboe after we'd gone to bed. My stepmother was patient and she ignored my moods. Papa had outbursts of affection. We left again, just the two of us. Our excitement didn't last long. There was just that one city in the middle of the countryside with wheat fields all around it. I asked him about Mama and Jimmy and London. I was afraid that he'd forget about my childhood. I remembered the nights when he'd leave for the nightclub, and it was like heaven for me. I was sorry I'd ever begged him to take me to America.

"I trained as a nurse. Maria wanted me to get married. She was afraid I'd go away and leave Papa behind. I'd seen an ad for the Red Cross. I left a letter on the table and went away in the middle of the night. Very romantic. And I ended up here. The Islands were the first stop in my trip around the world!"

The nurse, her eyes half closed, was laughing heartily. With the back of her hand, she wiped away the mascara that was running down from her eyelids. She was still sitting very erect, holding her empty glass—a boisterous schoolgirl waiting to be punished.

"What about your father?"

"He'd phone me when he'd been drinking. He didn't know what to say. I'd ask if he still played the oboe. He died a few years later, of cirrhosis."

Strange fate, thought François Robidoux. She'd exchanged a prison of wheat fields in Saskatchewan for an island battered by the Atlantic. Mainlanders who lived on the Islands must share a peculiar inner fate.

"Were you the first nurse to work here?"

"Nurse Boudreau was here before me."

"Boudreau?"

"She was a Boudreau from Havre-Aubert. Her mother was Irish, she spoke English. She was glad when I turned up."

"Why did you stay?"

She shrugged.

"The first winter was rough. There was meningitis. One child died, another was left deaf. Bill came to see me every day. He'd do favours for me. He was— funny. He had a funny approach to life, as if he knew he'd be dead at thirty-eight. At first it was a game. After that we had to get married. Whenever I talked about travelling he'd just laugh. The children came. And that's it."

"What an amazing life," said Robidoux. "In 1958, at the age of twenty, to come to Entry Island as a nurse!"

"You think that's interesting?"

Mrs. Patterson bent down and took a black notebook from a drawer.

"My diary. You may find this entertaining."

"Are you really lending it to me?"

"Aren't we good friends?"

The wind had dropped. A sliver of moonlight slipped in through the window. The nurse's account had drained her last reserves of lucidity. She was drunk, staring vacantly, gesturing vaguely.

"What's keeping you here?" she asked.

"Nothing. I'm free. So why not stay another year or two?"

François didn't dare admit to the nurse that her story had stirred some haunting questions in him. What in fact was keeping him on this isolated archipelago? Why hadn't he gone back to the city with Gigi Bengale after his one-year stint? Had he traded the skirts of the university for those of the Atlantic? From the mainland he received only a feeble breeze, warmed by the Gulf Stream and by two hundred years of island tradition. He had his habits, friends, his work. Would he succumb to the charms of the pale dunes where so many ships had foundered? Among his patients' ancestors were numerous castaways who had run aground one stormy night and never left. Was he to be the starting point of one of those little families lost among flocks of LeBlancs and Arseneaus? Or would he end up an old bachelor in a bungalow overlooking Cap-aux-Meules?

"Look out for the island girls," murmured Mrs. Patterson. "They're witches."

"Really?"

The nurse didn't reply. She glanced out the window towards the lighthouse.

"I wonder what Father Jeffrey's up to. . . . That woman went to see him a while ago. She left with her bag after supper and told Phyllis not to worry if she didn't come back."

"Did she get to the lighthouse?"

"I saw her heading that way. I wonder what they're doing. . . . "

François didn't reply. He had the impression that his hostess was about to pass out over her plate. The bowtie was pinching his neck. All he wanted was a bed and a book.

"I'm going home to sleep now," he announced. "I've got a date with Timmy in the morning."

"Timmy! He's already forgotten. He talks a lot when he has a drink in his hand."

"Quite a character!"

The nurse looked at him sharply.

"Timmy Collins is a son of a bitch. I've never understood how he can paint."

"What makes you say that?"

"All his life he's taken advantage of people. Did you know that his wife had money? When he met her she'd just inherited some boarding houses in Toronto. She supported them while he was becoming a painter. As soon as his pictures started bringing in money, he threw it all overboard—wife, children. The people here know him very well."

François Robidoux said nothing. Should he be offended by these mean-spirited remarks? Wasn't every marriage a pact strewn with unreadable clauses? Creation wasn't accomplished by pure spirits. His work had taught him to respect his patients' shortcomings. Like bacteria, they ensured a balance in the personality's grey zones that was dangerous to disturb.

Mrs. Patterson sensed his reluctance to speak ill of Timmy Collins. She poured herself another drink.

"Stay here. It's a lot more comfortable than the clinic."

"I'd rather go."

Robidoux's voice was shaking. Mrs. Patterson looked at him morosely and sighed. Then she got up and tacked towards the bathroom, where she began to gather up the doctor's clothes. He heard a sound like a gong.

He rushed to the bathroom. The nurse was on her knees in front of the dryer, rubbing her forehead. François didn't dare laugh. Mrs. Patterson would never forgive him for seeing her in this condition. She was trying unsuccessfully to fold his trousers.

"François?"

"Yes."

"I'm drunk. I'm sorry. I'm an old fool."

"You're perfectly normal. It's Hallowe'en. Never mind the pants."

She stood up. She was smiling between half-closed eyes. With dread in his heart, François helped her up to her bedroom.

He let the nurse collapse onto her bed. She was offering formless apologies in which the words Timmy and bastard were entangled. He put a cold cloth on her forehead. She pulled him onto the bed.

"Stay with me. Just tonight. Nobody has to know. . . . You can leave before dawn. . . . No one will know, just you and me. What difference does it make if you sleep over at an old fool's?"

François Robidoux stayed beside her, motionless. He gazed at her neck which was streaked with parallel wrinkles, like floodlines. Mrs. Patterson had her eyes closed, to avoid looking at him. Why not sleep with this woman? He'd gone up to her bedroom. What would it be like to make love with a woman of fifty? What would their relations be afterwards?

He rose hesitantly. The nurse sat on the edge of the bed, holding onto him by the hips.

"Stay a while."

He stood like a statue, gasping and frightened. With shaking hands she undid his belt and pulled down his pants. His sex hesitated, half-swollen under his briefs. She grasped it with her big hand. It hardened, abandoning Robidoux on the shores of his indecision.

"You see...."

She pulled down his briefs.

Chapter 10
Nothing's More Suspect Than Good Intentions

Anchored between Mrs. Patterson's heavy thighs, François Robidoux felt useless, like the male of a matriarchal species. He was advancing into the depths of an endless vagina, stealthily entering a hostile forest. The nurse, indifferent, was drifting towards some memory, noisily, to the accompaniment of spasmodic little sobs. He felt numbed by alcohol, his penis like lead, foreign. The woman's white body undulated, immense and mysterious. Orgasm eluded him. Feeling himself go limp, he withdrew.

For a moment Mrs. Patterson didn't move, her high-pitched voice still moaning. Then she brought her hand to her belly and caressed herself, pinching her lips.

François Robidoux watched her, hypnotized. He became aware of his state. The wedding tie felt tight around his neck and his shirt was hanging out, half unbuttoned. The bedroom reeked of wine and sweat. How could he have let the old alcoholic bewitch him? By dawn, the whole island would know.

"Come here."

The nurse was holding out her hand. Robidoux backed up to the door. Mrs. Patterson slumped onto the bed, where she sank into a half-sleep. He raced downstairs and hastily changed his clothes. A glass of wine was depositing a yellow halo on the cover of the nurse's diary. He grabbed the book and left.

A lamp came on in Mrs. Patterson's bedroom. She looked out the window at him. He stammered a ridiculous "Good morning," and headed for the clinic.

The hay was undulating in the breeze. Shards of light burst from the houses. In the distance, two trucks went clattering over ruts and potholes. The party was still in progress. Outside the lighthouse, he spied the silhouette of the unknown woman as she was turning onto the road to the church. Walking slowly and deliberately, she resembled a scholar-monk philosophizing in a cloister. François slowed down. The woman was bringing a shiny object to her mouth: the water pipe he'd glimpsed on the ferry.

"Hello," she said simply. "I saw you this morning."

She pronounced the word "saw" as if she had X-ray vision.

"Nice night, isn't it?"

"Fantastic," she muttered, shifting her interest to her pipe. "Want a hit?"

She exhaled a blue cloud and offered him the pipe. Robidoux hesitated. He hadn't smoked since college, on the advice of his great-uncle, a doctor, who had warned him about "narcotics" when he started medical school. The storm had cut him off from the world. Boarding the *Gertrude-Béatrice* this morning, he'd opened, just a crack, a door through which all the winds of autumn had come rushing out.

He pulled on the pipe and a gurgling sound travelled from its steel belly to his brain.

"Granola," he thought, "she's a refugee from the sixties."

They introduced themselves. She told him her name was Margie.

"Margie Stone," she specified.

They giggled.

"You were at the lighthouse?" he asked.

"I went to see Jeffrey Ballantyne."

"You know Father Jeffrey?"

"I'm his wife."

François choked. Margie Stone looked at him proudly.

"Congratulations. I didn't know he was married."

"God! We aren't actually married. I'm divorced."

"You don't live together?"

"He's afraid of what people will say. But it'll happen. Tomorrow, next week—or five years from now."

"You'll wait as long as you have to, is that it?"

"Sure! I came here to be with him for good. To hell with them!"

"To hell with them!"

"And what are you doing on this island? You're the doctor, right?"

"I'm stuck because of the wind. I can't leave."

"A lot of the people here are prisoners of the wind."

François Robidoux felt a heaviness creep along his neck and his limbs. In a subtle way, time was expanding. Their words ruffled the night, like pieces on a chessboard. Each phrase brought in its wake a full range of possible meanings. Feverishly, François extracted the most plausible, though he didn't feel that he could trust it. It was exhausting.

"Good thing I brought warm clothes," the woman added after a silence.

"I didn't bring anything. And the wind can blow for days."

"What's that you've got?"

"The diary of a nurse who came here thirty years ago."

"Sounds heavy. . . . You don't look like an ordinary doctor."

"I am, though, a very ordinary one. I take care of

people who want to die and don't have the guts to admit it."

"God, Doctor! You're too serious. People want to live, not die. They shouldn't. Death is the biggest trip. Hash is nothing in comparison."

They'd arrived at the clinic.

"You don't mind that Jeffrey won't marry you?"

"Not in the least. Unhappiness is behind me. I don't have any more time. I'm forty-one years old. See you tomorrow."

"Tomorrow?"

"We'll see each other tomorrow. The island's small. We're prisoners of the wind. The wind can blow for days. You said so yourself."

She gave him her angelic look. Damned witch, he thought. Nothing's more suspect than good intentions. He had a tender thought for Mrs. Patterson, sleeping it off up there near the cliffs.

Chapter 11
Miss Hadfield

François Robidoux strode as far as the clinic. In a bedroom there he found a threadbare dressing gown and put it on; he looked like a ruined baron. Solemnly, he inspected the three bedrooms, then went downstairs, checked the locks, and turned out the lights. After that he got into bed and opened the diary. The binding creaked. The tops of some pages had recently been torn. The nurse seemed to have reread it a short time ago, after leaving it in a damp spot for years.

29 September 1958
About fifty people were waiting on the wharf for me this morning. The mayor, a big surly man, helped me disembark. The islanders stared at me in silence. I felt as if I was getting out of a stagecoach to go into a saloon.

The mayor drove me to the clinic in his buggy. A giggling horde of blond children chased after us. Sitting very erect in my seat, I had a view of the sea all around me. I was balanced on a twenty-five-cent piece floating on the ocean.

The houses are a pitiful sight with their grey shingles and dilapidated sheds. The gardens are well maintained, with fences around them to keep animals out. The clinic is in a house at the bottom of the hill. The mayor showed me inside. Some women were waiting for me, dressed in their Sunday best. The men brought in my trunks, the mayor introduced me to the ladies and disappeared without a word, his duty done.

My hostesses were charming. They showed me around, making a list of everything that needed fixing. I asked to see the doctor's office. Silence. They took me to an incredibly messy room. The instruments lay on a dusty tray. It was like walking into an illustration from my anatomy textbook. I'd have to write the Red Cross or the M.P., have some modern equipment sent on the next boat.

A buffet had been set out in the living room. As I was sitting down to eat, feeling better, a young boy stood in the doorway and coughed: his mother was going into labour. A Mrs. Dingwell got up. Since Nurse Boudreau's departure, she'd been helping any women who hadn't—to be on the safe side—crossed over to Cap-aux-Meules.

I was very keyed up when I ran to get my instruments. I asked where the fetoscope was. I'd only brought a stethoscope, sure I'd find the rest when I got here. The ladies were horrified. I tried to reassure them, even though I was quaking in my boots. What was this instrument I needed so badly? I was describing it, with great difficulty, when one of them remembered that three weeks before she'd seen a kid named Jeffrey playing with an odd-looking car horn. As for Mrs. Dingwell, she found it suspicious that I'd need this weird-sounding thingamajig for a confinement.

I was taken to the bedside of a red-headed woman who was having no trouble delivering a wild-eyed baby. Though I worried at how thin he was, the others thought he looked wonderful. Once everything was taken care of, we had nothing better to do than return to our meal at the clinic. Later, the fetoscope was found on a neighbour's scarecrow. Young Jeffrey's mother offered to buy me a new one, but I'd rather hang onto this one. No instrument, not even the most modern, will let me do a better job of listening to the hearts of Entry Island babies.

I bought this diary in Montreal, thinking of all the long evenings waiting for me. I'm the nurse at this outpost in the middle of the Atlantic. The wind has dropped. The silence now is supernatural. I wanted to be alone. And here I am.

6 October 1958

Wrote to Dad yesterday. It's been over two weeks since I left Saskatoon. He must be worried. It felt good, knowing I'd made my escape. That simple note on the table: "I've gone to see the world. Gladys". Banal but exhilarating. When he gets my letter he'll be able to locate me in the universe. I'll exist in one precise and mysterious place: ENTRY ISLAND, MAGDALEN IS-LANDS, QUEBEC. He'll search his atlas but he'll only find a little fish-hook stuck in the throat of the St. Lawrence. He'll get up and take his oboe, or a gin, or both. He won't be able to sleep till he's answered me.

I was the one who asked him to bring me to America. Why do I need to punish that man who left everything behind for me?

8 October 1958

Tonight a woman took me to the bedside of her uncle, Clarence Aitkens. He'd fallen and cracked open his skull. The woman was worried about infection. On the way there she told me, with a mixture of pride and shame, that her uncle was a weird bird. Among other things, he had never let Nurse Boudreau into his house. Ten years ago he'd chosen to put his broken wrist between two planks rather than go to the hospital.

"He's been like that since the war."

"For fifteen years?"

"Forty years! Since the Great War."

"Does he live alone?"

"He's a bachelor."

The cabin was tiny. He was lying on a faded sofa. When we arrived he turned to face the wall.

"Get out!"

The woman put down her coat and started tidying the counter that served as his kitchen.

"That cut's liable to get infected, Clarence. Nurse Hadfield's going to sew you up."

"Get the bitch out of here."

I prepared to leave.

"A cup of tea, Miss Hadfield?"

The woman glared at me. Apparently I was supposed to stay.

"Gladly."

I sat down to withstand the siege. The niece, impassive, made the tea and took a seat beside me.

"Do you want a cup, Clarence?"

"Go to hell."

We sipped our tea in silence. The old man ignored us. The room smelled of spruce. After twenty minutes I plucked up my courage and went over to the patient. At the top of his grimy hair was a gaping cut three inches long, coated with some sticky substance I couldn't identify.

"Spruce gum," observed my accomplice in a neutral tone.

"How old are you, Mr. Aitkens?" I asked stupidly.

"Figure it out for yourself!"

Emboldened, I came closer and put my finger on his skull. Suddenly I was looking at a face that was almost hidden by a yellowish beard. He pointed to a rifle hanging on the wall.

"See that gun? Get out!"

He stared at me with his baboon's eyes. Slowly, I

retreated towards the door and picked up my things. I was afraid he'd shoot me down without a trial, like a Prussian. The niece was as calm as before.

"Don't be an idiot, Clarence. That's a nasty cut and it's going to get infected."

I stayed in the doorway. Old Clarence lay down again, facing the wall.

"I'll come back tomorrow, Mr. Aitkens."

18 October 1958
I've thought a lot about Dad's letter.

"I couldn't ask you at the age of nine to come right out and say that you didn't want me to remarry. I should have figured it out by myself. You waited till you turned twenty, and then you got tired of resisting and left on your own. I can't blame you for that."

Such resignation worries me. Why did I abandon him, on the threshold of old age, in Saskatoon, that strange city? I could have been the one to bring *him* to America.

He'd have refused to go.

22 October 1958
All week, the east wind lashes furiously at the island. I listen to my patients' conversations: the east wind brings rain, storms, changes of season. It carries the North Atlantic clouds, the damp breath of the high autumn seas. The west wind is an earth wind, bearer of fine weather.

The ferry hasn't come for three days now. The island has shrunk into its carapace. People run from house to house, small blurry silhouettes inside their oilskins. They drink and play cards. They work a little, fix traps that were broken during the fishing season. For the first two days they seemed to forget me. Not one visit, not a single phone call. I wandered through all the drafty rooms. The first day, I dressed myself from head to toe. On the second, I stayed in my housecoat. I had to put towels under my bedroom window, turn on the oil stove. I read everything that was lying around the house—cheap paperback novels, almanacs, cookbooks. I found an anatomy textbook. *Teres major, flexor carpi ulnaris, pectoralis minor. . . .* I memorized the nineteen muscles of the forearm and the eight division branches of the internal carotid artery.

The phone rang at eight o'clock this morning. Phyllis Dickson, the mayor's wife, was worried about me. The weather was atrocious. The rain was dripping from my bedroom under the wallpaper into the kitchen.

Ten minutes later, someone burst through the porch. A strapping young fellow, soaking wet and holding his sou'wester, looked at me delightedly.

"Morning. I'm Bill."

He crushed my fingers in his icy hand. I asked if anything was wrong. He chuckled. My question seemed to remind him of something comical.

"Everything's fine, miss. Where are they?"

"What?"

"Your storm windows."

He laughed again. Without even bothering to take off his boots, he tramped down to the cellar. It was clear that he knew where to look for the windows. He walked awkwardly and his bovine face was lit up by the rain.

"You're going to put them up in this weather?"

"Can't let you freeze in this stable, miss."

He had a comical way of emphasizing the word "miss". I went upstairs to change and tidy up. The man perilously put up the window in my bedroom. He sang to himself in the wind to impress me. When he put up the downstairs windows he left his ladder against the house.

"I'll come back for the others when the wind dies down. Your oil tank's just about empty. Better order some more."

He stood in the doorway smiling, waiting for a reply. And chuckled again when I asked how much I owed him.

"Two sugars, one milk."

"You'll have to make do with the sugar. I'm out of milk."

"I'll bring you some, don't worry."

"I'm not worried. Coming in?"

He sat awkwardly at the kitchen table and answered my questions with sibylline little phrases. I thought I understood him to say that in Nurse Boudreau's time, he did the maintenance work around the clinic. He lives near the lighthouse, with his parents. His embarrassment was growing by the minute. He gulped his third cup of tea and excused himself, pleading some job to do for his father.

"Do you have that much to do today?"

"There's always work to be done, miss."

He laughed one last time and disappeared into the rain. Had I annoyed him with my questions? I'll be more careful in future.

4 November 1958

For the past week the silence in the house has seemed not so heavy. I'm delighted to come back to it from my house calls. In the midst of this emptiness I feel as if I really exist. Among these strangers I'm becoming myself as much as it's possible to be anything other than a sum of influences. Which is a fancy way to say that I'm learning to live alone.

A few flakes of snow have fallen. I'm awaiting the winter with a mixture of eagerness and apprehension.

For my birthday, Phyllis Dickson bought me some wool and taught me how to knit. I laughed when she showed up with her grandmotherly paraphernalia.

"You're really afraid I'll be bored, Mrs. Dickson."

"A nurse ought to know that prevention's easier than curing."

She's taken me under her wing. She has no daughters. I remind her of her youth. She envies me.

In the evening, I curl up on a sofa in front of the wood stove that Bill, my other guardian angel, has set up. Back home from a rural house call, I slip into a daydream. I review the day's events, see again my life in Saskatoon, I invent peculiar stories, blazing loves. I'm a southern heiress awaiting disaster in the silence of a plantation.

I worry that I won't be able to adjust to the constraints of a family or marriage when I go back. Solitude is like a fire: approach it and you get warm, come a little closer and you get burned.

6 November 1958

Since Clarence Aitkens threw me out, I've gone to see him twice a week. The first time, I just left some iodine and bandages on the table. "Good morning, Mr. Aitkens. I'll be back on Monday."

The second time, the cabin was empty. Someone had cleaned up. The tins of food were lined up on the shelves. Clarence or his niece had wiped off the table and replaced the bottle and bandages where I'd put them. I left a note on the table and went on my way.

This game has been going on for four weeks now. The hermit clears out when I come near, or else he refuses to open his door.

This morning I found him at home, splitting wood. When he saw me coming he pulled down his tuque.

"Good morning, Mr. Aitkens."

Paying no attention to me, the old man split a log with exaggerated vigour. I sat down, off to the side. At least he hadn't chased me away. He took another log, a massive one with a knot running through it. The axe went into the centre, but it didn't even make a dent. One stroke of the axe, two strokes, three. He was breathing very hard.

"What if you turned it?"

He put down the axe and gave me a nasty look. He got his breath back.

"You want to try?"

"I'm sure you'll get there."

He brought down the axe with all his might. His tuque went flying under the shock, uncovering his wound now painted with iodine. A timid crack had opened in the log.

"You lost your tuque, Mr. Aitkens."

The old man shook the shavings off his hat. He smiled faintly. Chalk one up for me.

24 December 1958

Three days of glorious weather. The northwest wind has left a thick layer of snow. The island has been abandoned to the animals and sleighs. The men have been putting the final touches on their barrels of moonshine, the women are baking mounds of pies and cakes, the children spend all day sliding down hills.

Holiday visiting is under way. Despite my protests, Bill Patterson has given me two forty-ouncers of gin.

"What'll you offer people, miss, when they come calling?"

I'm glad he warned me. People turn up at any hour, four or five at a time, and don't leave till they've tasted my elixir. A few stops along the stations of the cross leaves them the worse for wear. They'll stop at a house, sleep, play cards, then leave so they can begin again.

That goes on for two weeks, till the supplies run out.

Bill invited me to his parents' house for Christmas. I said no. He seemed more puzzled than disappointed.

"You aren't going to celebrate Christmas here all by yourself?"

He hates being alone. He's always looking for someone to tell a story to, some job to be done, a soul to help out. An islander. It's hard for him to understand my reluctance to get involved in community parties. He drops in whenever he feels like it, without knocking. When I told him the clinic wasn't a shed he apologized, ironically calling me "miss." Would he have to submit to scheduled visits? Invent diseases?

"You're sick enough as it is, Bill Patterson."

The next minute we were laughing our heads off. He exasperates me with his stories and his gossip. There are times, though, when I'm glad to hear his heavy steps.

"How's it going, miss?"

Very well. So well that I turned down his invitation.

25 December 1958

I spread a white cloth on the kitchen table, a lovely, brand-new one I've just received from Montreal. Having no wine I opened the second bottle of gin. To hell with visitors! I'd set two places, carefully. He'd arrive at any moment, with his oboe under his arm. The lamb was delicious. Phyllis had made me some real mint sauce. I could see the sleighs around the church. During Mass, the men stood at the windows, which were open a crack, so they could keep an eye on their horses.

I didn't have any music. Nurse Boudreau promised to bring me a record-player from Halifax. I had to be satisfied with the crackling of wood in the stove. Your good health, Dad. Do you remember our first Christmas, in the apartment in London? I was six years old.

I can see you very clearly. You told me it would be our last wartime Christmas. You'd said that the year before, too, but this time I almost believed you. Every week you took out a map of Europe to show me the Allies' progress. They were in Belgium now. Somehow or other they were getting close to Berlin and the place where the Germans launched their rockets. Why had a rocket, launched blindly from a Baltic forest, landed—out of all the houses on our street, in Chelsea, in London, or in England—why had it landed on our house just as Mummy was giving Jimmy his piano lesson? Why hadn't they come to the park with us? Chance. Who is chance? Nobody. Is it a thing? No, it was neither a person nor a thing. When Miss Oates stuck her hand in the hat at school, no one knew what name she would draw. My mother and my brother were crushed by chance, which was neither a person nor a thing. Someone had drawn their names from a big hat.

You changed the subject. You showed me the cities you'd take me to see when the war was over. You've always liked maps, Dad. You should have been a geographer. Then you wouldn't have had to play the tango afterwards, in the dance halls.

I couldn't have cared less about Vienna or the war. That night, in an apartment filled with merrymakers' shouting, behind shutters closed for the curfew, you carved the lamb and gave me my first glass of wine, horrible wine you'd paid a fortune for on the black market. Your cheeks were red, you were smiling, and you didn't stop talking. There were four of us at the table. That night I told myself that chance, the hand in the tall hat, could only be God. The God-child in his stable in Bethlehem. The wine made me sick to my stomach.

The phone rang on the stroke of midnight. Dad had

calculated the time difference between Saskatoon and the Maritimes. Merry Christmas. Merry Christmas. This was the first one we weren't spending together. We'll make up for it next year. Yes, Daddy. He was trying to be cheerful. He must have had a drink with some customers. Maria was cooking their Christmas dinner, Hans had gone out. He'd be back for midnight. Unless he forgot about it in a bar.

The connection was poor. I pictured the telephone cable running along the bottom of the Gulf, eighty miles to Cape Breton, in the sand and mud, between the crabs and phosphorescent fish. Then its course from pole to pole, as far as that small town in Saskatchewan, lying frozen under the Arctic winds. We were too far away. The curfew has been lifted. The London apartment lost its magic somewhere between England and America. The war is over now. Above us there are only fields of stars, as far as the eye can see. Our world was shattered long ago, Daddy.

He was shouting at the other end of the line. The roar of a blizzard was growing louder in my ears. Hundreds of voices were nibbling at the net of sound that was making its way to me. I wished him one last "Merry Christmas" and hung up.

The lamb was cold but I was hungry and ate it anyway. And drank a fair amount of gin. I walked all over the house, leaning on the door-posts, listening to the sleigh bells outside. That first Christmas in the London apartment, Dad finished off the bottle of wine. I was sick to my stomach. He gave me baking soda, which made me vomit, then he washed me off, dried me carefully, and put me in his bed, where he read to me till two in the morning. He fell asleep with his nose in the story-book. Even though it was Christmas there was an air-raid warning. I opened the shutter, thinking that Santa Claus would never come down with all this racket. Dad was asleep. Why wake him up? If a rocket landed on us we'd join Mother and Jimmy. I took away his book and his glasses and lay down beside him.

A team was approaching. The sound of sleigh bells grew louder in the night. I heard the porch, then familiar footsteps.

"Miss! Are you asleep?"

9 January 1959
Fatigue is gnawing at me and I feel like crying. What on earth was I thinking of, when I buried myself away here? I don't have a missionary's soul. This is no place for a single woman. I could stay here ten years, but I'd never be one of them.

22 January 1959
This morning a boat managed to take little James to Cap-aux-Meules. He was half-conscious and burning with fever in spite of the penicillin injections. The hospital may be able to save him. I'm tired. I spent the night at his bedside, listening to the wind outside to see if they'd be able to make the crossing. He was adrift in his bed. There were black spots scattered over his cheeks and body and he was weak, his pulse racing, suspended in a limbo from which I couldn't rescue him. He was breathing, though, easily and evenly. I couldn't take my eyes off his mouth, afraid the air would stop coming out. Hold on, little boy, hold on now.

There wasn't anything else I could do. I called Dr. Bailly. He sighed, told me the dosages, didn't hold out much hope. Meningococcal infection. I've seen the name in my books. I should send him all the children who might be infected.

Around four o'clock the little boy went into convulsions. After that he fell into a deeper sleep, refusing to swallow anything. I waited for the sun to come up. Old Dr. Bradley used to say that children draw new strength from it. Hang on, James, hang on there. Your father's next door in the kitchen. He and your uncles have stayed up together. They won't sleep till they know you're all right. James. Your name is the same as my brother's, who died. Don't leave me. Push your chest out one more time. That's it. Look, the sun is coming up. You're breathing easier now. Your fever has dropped. The men go down to the wharf to see if the ice has moved. You'll be leaving for the hospital soon.

In two hours, when the boat's in open water, I'll be able to breathe. After that, things will be outside my jurisdiction. Bill takes me back to the clinic. Tears are drying on my cheeks. He tells me silly jokes. No miserable little meningitis is going to get the better of a McPhail. He thinks I'm crying for the child.

5 February 1959
Little James is back from the hospital, as bright as ever. The whole island came to see him. Gloria stayed at home, inconsolable. Why had James, the youngest of nine children, survived, when her only son had died? Why do children die?

I don't want to have children.

27 February 1959
The days are getting longer. The men are feverish. They scan the horizon, question the winds, prepare their dories for the seal hunt. Bill seems to have a new lease on life. He goes to bed and gets up early, shuts himself away in his stable to prepare his rigging. He goes up to the lighthouse every day for endless conversations with the keeper about the movement of the ice floes. He wouldn't prepare for a holy war any more carefully.

He takes me to the edge of the promontory, teaches

me the vocabulary of the ice. I can't understand their interest in this hunt. I asked Bill if it was the danger that attracted him. He guffawed.

"You don't get it at all, miss."

"Why risk your life for a few sealskins and two hundred dollars?"

"No reason."

"What is it then?"

He shrugged. The tribe is preparing for a ritual. It has nothing to do with me.

2 March 1959

Phyllis woke me up early this morning. The men were gathering at the Southwest Point. The seal were in sight, south of Bout du Banc.

For two days now the dories have been waiting on the beach. The men were grouped in squads of five. The other islanders stood on shore, following their departure. The hunters slung ropes over their shoulders and hauled the heavy fishing boats into the sea. Beyond the shore ice, a thin crust of crushed ice lay over the treacherously sighing sea. Islets of various shapes and sizes were adrift in this mush. Farther out to sea, stretches of open water gleamed among the compact masses of the ice floes, coming together, spreading apart, according to the winds and currents. The tide was nudging this chaos into the channel. Dents formed in the masses of ice, then they rose up and split apart with a muffled rustling that sounded, from the shore, like murmurs from the coupling of monstrous beasts.

The men made their way out towards this underside of the world. Slanting sunlight set fire to splinters on the peaks of the broken-up ridges. Without even a glance in my direction, Bill took his place in the middle of his squad. The hunters, starting with Bill, reminded me of children playing war. The same serious expressions, the same implacable will, the same bogus stakes. In April, they'd all go back to fishing, back into the skins of reasonable men. While they waited, they would go out on the ice, masters and lords, to play at games of life and death.

The crowd dispersed. On the shore ice, the older men used binoculars to follow the movements of the ice and the squads. The day stretched out slowly. In every house the hunt was the only topic of conversation. The women talked about it with chilly respect, as if it were a strange woman to whom they lent their husbands once a year. They took me in with new familiarity. Because of Bill, I shared their anxiety. This conspiratorial atmosphere was getting on my nerves.

Around four o'clock the first squads appeared on the horizon. They were approaching slowly, the men bracing themselves against dories laden with pelts to the gunwales, pulling, pushing, falling exhausted into the traps of the frazil ice. The light was rapidly disappearing. The glacier was springing back to life, weary of these insolent men who had ventured onto its surface. The islanders rushed to the edge of the hill, ready to welcome the men and to pull the boats onto the beach. Behind their frozen beards the hunters laughed. They'd take a swig and proudly count their skins.

I stood off to one side. The wind turned northwesterly and spread out, stirring up torrents of snow that stung my eyes. Two squads, one of them Bill's, had not come in. I was worried. Phyllis came over to me. I knew the stories. Some men had spent the night on the ice, taking shelter between their boats and the low walls of seals. Others had drifted into the Gulf and never returned. It took only the smallest thing, a change in the wind or the current, a breakdown.

Night was falling. Fires were lit on the beach. A dory appeared in the dimness. It wasn't Bill's. They'd been sighted five hundred feet to the south. They should be here at any minute. I shifted restlessly before the fire, frozen stiff and furious.

We heard voices and the creak of a boat on the ice. It was pitch-black now. Ghosts drew near, wrapped in a coating of ice that the drifting snow made heavier by the minute. The old people nodded. They'd been very foolhardy.

At the head of the squad, Bill was pulling hard at the oars. He looked more like a bear than ever. As he stepped onto terra firma, he glanced my way. I stalked off in the direction of the clinic.

Now he's just dropped in to see me, freshly washed but still smelling of seal. He was more serious than usual, or more tired. He stood in the porch waiting for me to ask him in. He'd been drinking.

I told him I wanted to go to bed early. He stayed put, trying to find something funny to tell me. I had to ask him to leave.

I'm not in love with Bill Patterson. I didn't come to this island to develop a crush on a lobster fisherman.

With heavy eyes, François Robidoux leafed through the diary. About thirty pages left. Dear Mrs. Patterson! What a road she'd travelled. ... He looked around him. Was it in this bedroom that she'd plunged into her anatomy book? Was this the window Bill Patterson had changed?

Someone was sounding a car horn in the night. François Robidoux put down the diary and switched off the light.

Chapter 12
Ulysses

The phone rang in his sleep, then in reality. Two-thirty a.m. Robidoux thought that Eva Patton had heaved her final sigh.

"Doctor?"

He recognized Charlene Collins.

"I've got something important to tell you."

"At this hour of the night?"

"I'll be on the wharf at three o'clock, on board the *Melinda D.*"

She hung up.

That was a good one. François laughed and went back upstairs to curl up under the covers.

The brief conversation left him wide awake. I'll be on the wharf at three o'clock, on board the *Melinda D. . . . .* Would Charlene lend herself to a practical joke? What if she was telling the truth? If she was really making a date with him? Could he imagine anything more romantic than meeting Charlene Collins on a boat, under the October moon? He'd never forgive himself for missing such an opportunity.

François Robidoux M.D. left the warmth of his bed and set off for the harbour. The road was deserted. From the southeast a quartering wind urged him on towards the wharf. His mind was clear, having shed the aftermath of alcohol and hashish.

The prospect of a tête-à-tête with Charlene filled him with apprehension. The first time she'd called him, he'd been charmed by her voice. Beneath the courtesy she sounded brisk and curious. She seemed more interested in the tone of what he said than in the content. When he'd first met her at her father's house he'd been captivated, but he maintained his professional reserve. He found in her the irony of old man Collins. She and her father lived in a world of their own, a product of dream and of childhood. He didn't want to give the impression that he was trying to enter it.

Their phone calls had taken on a familiar turn. She called more frequently, and his replies were longer than they should have been. The painter's aches and pains became a pretext for informal battles of wits. Robidoux had come to look forward to these weekly oases. Moved by sound instinct, the hospital switchboard operator stopped screening Charlene's calls, transmitting them with resigned discretion no matter where he was in the building.

These exchanges occurred on the fringe of his affair with Gigi Bengale, in a compartmentalized world adjoining his work. If asked about it, Robidoux would have taken offence with fine candour, so improbable did his complicity with Charlene seem to him. The girl was confused with Entry Island: she disappeared into the mist without a warning. Since Gigi's departure, he often walked Freud on the beach. He'd look at the island off shore. He had to beware of a lively imagination that was exacerbated by celibacy. He picked up a hunk of wood and threw it into the waves. The dog just stood there, impassive. Why had he named it Freud?

Now she was calling him to come to her. He felt himself victim of an exaltation that reminded him a little of the first time he'd gone out with Gigi Bengale.

Did love consist of rolling a single stone, like Sisyphus, to the summit of his illusions? Margie Stone was right: he was too serious for his years. Unless he changed he was going to develop an ulcer or some psychosomatic illness that would show the whole world the canker of his insecurity.

"How about a little frivolity," he murmured through clenched teeth.

He passed the Anglican church and the graveyard. The white stones stood, lopsided, on the flanks of a low hill. The family names—Welsh, Dickson, Collins, Patton, McLean, Josey—were being eroded by the salt wind. Under the names of most of the men, the simple epitaph: *An able seaman.* Under the women's, a few tender words that were hidden by the damp grass.

His supper with Mrs. Patterson slept at the bottom of some glaucous water from which precise images rose. Crazy. The woman was crazy. The other one, on the road, the sixties throwback with her water pipe, wasn't much better. As for him, he was on his way, on this Hallowe'en night, to meet a siren with tawny hair.

Soon François Robidoux had come to the port. A truck with its hood pointing towards Cap-aux-Meules stood guard on a higher hill that towered over the pier. He left the road, drove along the beach strewn with seaweed and the debris of lobster traps, then onto the deserted wharf. Furious waves ruffled by the contrary winds splashed him with sea spray. The boats on their moorings lolled from side to side.

He knew the *Melinda D.* The blue boat belonged to Charlene's uncle. He boarded it. The cabin was locked; not a sign of life. His watch read five minutes to three. He jumped into another boat and, hidden behind a windlass, surveyed the entrance to the wharf. An automobile drove along the road to the church, then stopped fifty metres from the truck. Its lights went out. He heard doors open and close. He panicked. Men were going to appear and the whole thing would look ridiculous. The lobster was in the trap. Dear Charlene! . . . And Mrs. Patterson, with her talk about witches!

A silhouette approached the truck. François Robidoux heard a drunken cry. The shadow headed for the automobile, then immediately drove away.

There was no movement around the truck. A drunk sleeping it off before going home? François Robidoux breathed more comfortably. He waited some more. The boat smelled of beer and cod. The dampness went right through him.

Three-twenty. Not a sign of Charlene Collins. He couldn't wait to see what she'd look like at her father's house the next day. With a few curses and tremendous precaution he walked past the boats, picked his way towards the slip and into the fields through the dump. If anyone had seen him they'd talk for years about how he'd been seen at the dump on Entry that night.

He returned to the clinic, heading into the wind. The ceiling light in his bedroom wasn't working. Shivering, his legs like rubber, he slipped into bed. Out of the blue, a hand pinched his side.

Chapter 13
The Birds in Hong Kong

As soon as the doctors discharge him, Timothy Collins hobbles down to the harbour. Sampans glide along the greasy water, between the destroyers and the troop carriers. His foot is painful. The island still exists, here where the water ends, on the other side of the Americas. He no longer feels any desire to go home. Yet he's alive, just a touch of malaria and the wound on his foot.

Exhausted, he sits down facing the wharf. The dock workers give him a shifty look. The boss leaves his work to offer him a beer. Timothy Collins has forgotten that he's on the victors' side. A sad victor. Captured on the second day of the conflict, after firing three bullets. And then the sun, rats, mosquitoes, shots, one friend after another buried in the jungle. His mind dead, straining towards the vague light at the end of the night. Total darkness, the absence of news, his trepidation in the face of those Americans who take over the camp like tourists and offer him cigarettes.

The beer makes his stomach ache. He takes out his dollars and leaves one for the Chinese man. Behind him, the men make a dash for his bottle. He walks along the sea in the direction of the women's quarter. The city is crawling with soldiers on a spree. He returns salutes half-heartedly. He retraces the labyrinth he travelled a thousand times as he lay on his straw pallet, sees again the low door near which the old man dozes over his pipe. Inside, the madam is fatter now. She looks at him through tired eyes. She doesn't recognize him.

"Woman?"

"Li?"

"She's gone. . . . Dead."

He sits down again. The madam is not so much upset as worried at the prospect of losing a customer.

"Other girls. . . . Young girls. . . . "

He doesn't reply. She takes him by the arm and leads him to a room in the back. He goes up the stairs behind a girl who is very young and as thin as he is. The rooms haven't changed. He demands the one that looks out on the yard. There are no birds now, or if there are they aren't singing.

The girl stands in the middle of the room and looks at him. He sits on the bed and points to her dress. She smiles and disappears behind the screen. When she comes back he hasn't budged. He points to a chair at the foot of the bed, then at her robe. She takes it off and stands there, her belly flat, breasts barely sprouted on her skinny chest. She sits on the chair. He tumbles onto the bed, eyes closed. The Chinese girl looks at him, tries to guess his desires. He doesn't move, doesn't look at her. She holds out her hand, grazes his scrawny leg. He moans and does not move. The blood pounds at his temples.

The day belonged to music and painting, the night to memories. Timothy Collins lay in his bed, one shoulder pierced by pain. Ever since he'd been denied access, at will, to five or six hours of sleep, he no longer saw the world the same way. The night, long since fraternal, had become a swamp he emerged from exhausted and filled with a sense of urgency. Beginning at dawn, he played music. From his dressing room he witnessed the breaking of the day. The men went down to the harbour, going furtively to their stables. The women were taking the wind under the clotheslines.

That night, he heard Charlene go downstairs and phone from the kitchen. A few words, then she hung up. His doctor was in, of course. With his good hand, Collins hoisted himself out of bed and slumped into his chair. He was at his telescope in time to see his sombrely clad daughter head through the fields for the harbour.

Now Collins turned his telescope towards the clinic. Thirty seconds later, François Robidoux appeared. He was on his way to the jetty, hands in his pockets. As he approached the beach he grew cautious and disappeared behind a dune.

The painter got back into bed. While still a child, Charlene used to wander off. A moment's inattention and she'd disappear, her little blonde head hidden by the fields of hay. Two minutes later a neighbour would call and tell them. His wife, already worn out by the first three children, asked him time and again to put up a fence. Stubbornly, he refused, preferring to spend the summer dabbling with his paints, his gaze wandering from his easel to the child, his eyes summoning her back when she slipped away towards dangerous places, feigning not to see her when she delightedly outsmarted him.

Today she was the only one of his children with whom he still had any ties. Was it fair? The others, in the tacit trial surrounding his divorce, had taken his wife's side, reproaching him, in the end, for his absence. Charlene had kept silent until the day she came to join him on the island.

If she weren't there, would he do these paintings? Timothy Collins had always hoped for—and dreaded —another experience of a watertight solitude, so he could abandon himself without illusion to his images.

Chapter 14
Acrobats

Galvanized by an adrenaline surge, François Robidoux howled and burst out of bed like a rocket. He landed in the corridor, naked, hair standing on end, paralysed by the waves of Charlene Collins' laughter that unfurled from the bedroom.

He glanced towards the bed. In the half-light her tawny mop of hair was shaking convulsively. Torn between relief and anger, he was finally overcome by nervous laughter.

"Miss Collins! . . . Hee hee. . . . Ho ho!"

"Doctor Robbydoo! . . . You look so funny!"

Still shaking with hiccups, he saw himself, pecker in the air, under the watchful eye of this Irish witch. He made a run for his pants, pulled them on the wrong way, and ended up on the floor. Another explosion of laughter. He finally solved the pants problem and took a dignified seat by the window.

Robidoux was seething. He was going to bombard her with questions, but thought better of it. Was this just the prelude to a more elaborate joke? Was someone going to pop in and take their picture? He had to find out what she really wanted.

She was watching him out of the corner of her eye, amused. No phone now, no chaperones. Robidoux's throat was dry. He sat on his hands to conceal their shaking. Her laughter welled up again.

"Is this a habit of yours—sleeping in other people's beds?"

"Only people I like."

"Did you come here to sleep with me?"

"Very perceptive. I knew you were when you figured out the paintings."

"That's a joke."

"You don't have a shred of self-confidence. It's part of your charm."

"Why did you arrange to meet me on the boat?"

"Because it was so romantic. And to find out if you really wanted to see me."

"Why didn't you come?"

"Borden Welsh's truck was at the wharf. I didn't want to compromise you."

Charlene looked at François, her cheek resting in her hand.

"Any more questions, Doctor?"

He crossed his legs, uncrossed them.

"I'm bugging you, right?" she asked.

"I feel like an idiot. I almost want to go to bed in the other room."

"Maybe that's not such a bad idea."

François Robidoux got into the first bed he found. His heart was pounding. This girl was peeling him like an orange. Several minutes passed. He took a deep breath. And then events took a less dramatic turn. He jumped out of the bed and went back to his own room.

Charlene Collins was smoking a cigarette.

"Feeling better now?" she asked.

"I've got out of the habit of celebrating Hallowe'en. It'll come back."

"Am I forgiven? What's the feminine form of macho?"

They laughed again. François got undressed and got into bed beside her.

"You smell of cinnamon."

"I was baking pies this afternoon."

Charlene's gestures, the muffled sound of her lips on the cigarette, the warmth of her skin, the corners of her mouth that rose to uncover her eye teeth, brought back other memories, other nights. They lay there side by side, like friends. Their meetings and phone conversations took on a new relief, like so many markers along a road they might have shared unbeknownst to either. Blindly, separately, each of them had woven a web whose centre was this unreal cube of wood that pitched and tossed between the compact masses of past and future.

She put her head on his shoulder. François Robidoux was still suspicious. It wasn't normal for a girl to enter his life so casually. Why did he feel as if he'd always known her? Had he been waiting for her, under the cover of his all too reasonable life? It was all illusion. The island was overwhelming him; the night, the storm, the sea, were shaking his certainties. This red-haired siren would vanish with the sun. He had only to approach her, to hold out his hand, and her love would run like sand between his fingers.

Charlene's face blocked the window. She was looking at him, serious now, engrossed in some memory of her own. There were fine lines slanting towards her temples, and white threads in her mop of hair. Her fleshy lips were chapped. She displayed her wounds, the blood was leaving her, like dreams, abandoning her to the reality of bones. You start out plump and saturated with water, then slowly you dry up and harden, you feel dense, reasonable, and very real, filled with the past, until you become a cold stone that is thrown to the ground.

"What are you thinking about?" she asked.

"Nothing. I'm tired, I guess."

She kissed him gently.

"I'll go if you want."

"Stay. You're quite impressive."

"You've never slept with an Anglophone before?"

"Too dangerous. I've thought about you a lot in the past two months. I've been looking forward to your phone calls."

She doused the lamp and her cigarette. The moon shone on a silver necklace around her neck. They proceeded like acrobats across the high wire that isolated them from feeling like strangers. Charlene sank into a troubled world run through with visions, launching from it incomprehensible messages. Her murmurs, her cries, uttered in the English language, which was so close yet so remote, fuelled his passion. At the centre of his love there burned, beneath a shield of lead, a pure kernel of hatred. She urged him to come nearer to that fire, to stoke it with his fear and his rebellion. Fastening her legs behind him, she brought them both to the edge of a cliff and they leapt, feet together, into a black sea studded with stars, to emerge sweating and breathless and stunned by what had happened.

They drifted with their desultory thoughts. The echoes of trucks were heard less frequently now. It seemed to François Robidoux that his thoughts were amazingly clear. He knew it would only last a few minutes. Charlene looked up at the ceiling, absorbed in a universe in which he was a mere satellite.

"It's like dying," she said.

"Don't say that. I'm afraid of death. Ridiculous, isn't it?"

"I was frightened too."

"And now?"

"I trust you. You know Plato's cave? Death is our cave. If we don't look beyond it, all we see are shadows."

"That's very impressive."

"It's the only thing I remember from my philosophy courses, that business about the cave."

"What are you doing on this island in the middle of nowhere?"

"My island's no more isolated than yours is. I've got my father, and all this space. I go walking on the hills. I meet only the cows and the cliffs. We live in a bubble. I guess that's what I need right now. I've found the little girl of my childhood."

"Don't you get bored?"

"Of course I do. People should be bored a lot more than they are. It gives weight to so many things. Is *your* life any more interesting, with your patients, your friends, your travels, your bars?"

"Sounds like you've known me for years."

"It isn't hard to see through you. It's another part of your charm."

"What were you doing in Toronto?"

"Nothing much. Am I still impressive?"

"It's getting worse. Mrs. Patterson warned me to watch out for island girls. They're all witches."

"It's Hallowe'en, Doctor. There are witches everywhere. Witches are very erotic. Did you read *The Witches of Eastwick*?"

"I don't read novels. I go for walks with my dog."

"Freud, right? You had to show off how clever you are."

"How do you know?"

"Mrs. Patterson told me."

"Do you talk with her often?"

"When she comes to visit Dad."

"I thought he didn't want to see her."

"She usually stays in the kitchen. Sometimes I talk him into seeing her and I go up to the studio with her."

"She's crazy."

"She's always been like that. There are plenty of

crazy people here. We don't need your conventions."

What would Charlene think if he told her he'd slept with the nurse five hours ago? He shuddered. That scene would take its place in his personal horror museum, between the time he'd wet the bed at Denis Goyette's house and the time Gigi Bengale had caught him in a bar with an ex-girlfriend.

The wind was coming up again. The house began to sigh once more.

"This is a strange night."

"It's Hallowe'en, Doctor."

"You're probably the kind of girl I could fall in love with."

"You can't fall in love, with me or anybody else. You're scared. When you kiss, your heart's not in it; you make love violently, so you'll think you're in love. You're always on the lookout, like an intruder."

"You're very hard. Was it all right for you?"

"Making love is always good. I really like you."

"Me too."

"Now hush. The sun will be up soon. I'm going back to my father's place. You'll get on the boat and I'll call you twice a week to talk about him, and you'll tell your friends about me and I'll be a pleasant memory when you're old and impotent."

"And when I come here?"

"When you come here you'll go around on a three-wheeler with Mrs. Patterson and I'll make faces at you from the window."

Smiling, she searched him with her eyes. He was tormented at the thought of not seeing her again. There had to be somebody in her life. A woman like her couldn't be unattached. She'd just given a Hallowe'en treat to a smooth-talking womanizer. It would soon be midnight and Cinderella was about to disappear in her pumpkin coach.

She could read his mind.

"You don't trust me, Doctor Robbydoo."

Someone knocked at the door. Immediately the world shrank. He slipped on a bathrobe and went downstairs. The knocking grew louder.

Chapter 15
The Roads of the Kingdom

A little creature, numb with cold, wearing a cap with earflaps, had its nose pressed against the glass. François Robidoux ushered in a sad-faced middle-aged man lost in a fleece-lined coat that made him look like a penguin. He smelled of alcohol and he was walking straight. With his sombre gaze and his hollow cheeks, he looked like a guerrilla straight out of Hollywood who'd come to the wrong shooting stage.

"It's starting to rain," he murmured.

The doctor merely stared at him reprovingly.

"I'm glad to find you in, Doctor. You probably don't know me. I'm Jeffrey Ballantyne. I'm sure you've heard of me."

He smiled contritely after each sentence, to dispel any possible misunderstanding.

"You're right, Mrs. Patterson has talked about you."

"Dear Gladys! She told you I was shut up in the lighthouse where all I did was drink?"

"That's pretty much what she said."

"She was right, as usual. Have you noticed, Doctor, that Mrs. Patterson is always right? Her wishes are God's will! Hee hee!"

Abruptly, his laughter stopped.

"How can I help you, Father Jeffrey?"

"You see, there's some discomfort in here—" he indicated a region between his waist and his chin.

"Since my late father passed away suddenly at fifty-three, two years after my mother. . . . "

François showed him into the examining room. The pastor sat on the edge of his chair, sweating and grinning broadly. He looked as if he was about to ask for the toilet. In his thin voice, he described some inconsistent symptoms, punctuating them with remarks about the weather. François examined him hurriedly and assured him that his discomfort was harmless.

"Now you'll have to excuse me, Father Jeffrey. I've got a big day tomorrow."

"I'm afraid you'll be spending it here, Doctor. Listen to that wind."

It was blowing harder than ever, and the wind was laden with a drizzling rain that sputtered onto the roof.

"Can I count on your discretion?" asked the priest.

"Of course."

Charlene must be getting impatient upstairs. She couldn't leave: the stairs were right across from the door to his examining room.

"Here it is," began the clergyman, crimson-faced. "I'm sure you realize that we men of the church are still . . . are still men."

François Robidoux nodded.

"I have reason to believe that I'm sick. For two months I've been totally impotent."

He looked up, wary of any sign of amusement on the doctor's part.

"You may feel that in my line of work it's not a serious problem. If you think about it, it could even be an advantage. But it's very upsetting and it's keeping me from carrying out my ministry the way I'd like to."

"It's a problem every man experiences once in his life."

Though intrigued by the man's sex life, François was cool to the priest's difficulties. He asked the usual questions and inspected the equipment, which, while modest, seemed to be in perfect running order. He tried to shoo away his patient by suggesting that he cut down on the booze and get some rest. It was only temporary, and was likely due to psychological factors he'd be glad to discuss another time.

Father Jeffrey was crestfallen.

"I certainly don't want to impose on you, but this problem's extremely important to me."

"You'll have to excuse me. I'm going back to bed."

François Robidoux stood up. Desperate, the priest fidgeted in his chair. He was about to say something when there was a rustling sound on the stairs, followed by the slamming of the front door.

"Did you hear that, Doctor?"

"It's the wind. The door slammed."

"Are you sure? What's the matter? Don't you feel well?"

"It'll pass. A touch of flu."

"I'm sorry to disturb you in the middle of the night," said the priest sorrowfully. "I'll be on my way."

"No, no. Go on. It doesn't matter now."

Sick at heart, François resumed his seat.

"Have you ever wondered what makes a young man choose the religious life?"

"No."

"In 1968 I was a hippie. I'd left home, dropped out of school. I was part of the underground culture in Halifax. My peers there were all the family I needed. I felt that the life I was living was quite unusual, but actually I've never been such a conformist. I lived— please don't smile—in a commune, on a farm outside of town. That's where I met Margie."

"The woman who was on the boat this morning?"

"Yes," sighed the pastor. "She arrived from Cape Breton one morning. A beautiful blonde, bursting with health. We were on the same wave-length. In those days I had a certain charm. I played the guitar. Everything was ruined when we went to bed. I was useless. We laughed about it but it didn't change. It happened with other girls too. Margie dropped me. I drifted into all kinds of drugs and esoteric practices. I thought I'd be impotent for ever. Then, after a few rough years, I discovered I had a vocation. The churches were empty, they'd take anybody. So that solved my problem—besides giving me a way to make a living.

"Years later, in Halifax, I met an old prostitute. She asked me up to her place and I went because I had a hunch. Sure enough, after fifteen years of impotence, this time I didn't have the slightest trouble. A few days later I tried it out with another woman; I was cured. Better than cured, I was a stallion, as if all those years of abstinence had only whetted my appetite.

"Since then, I've been seeing the whore from Halifax once a month. She brings me luck. She's old now, but she does it as a favour, as if I were a child. Since I've been cured I've had only one thought in mind: to get back together with Margie. I did research, looked in all the phone books, then I finally found her by bribing someone in the tax department. She was married to a teacher and living in Sydney, with three grown-up children. I got myself assigned to a parish near her house.

"I wanted our reunion to have the beauty of chance. I spied on her comings and goings. She spent the mornings doing housework in her bungalow. You can imagine how I felt when I found the love of my youth transformed into a housewife. Her obvious boredom when she was watering her tulips reassured me. Afternoons, she divided her time between tai chi lessons and an environmental pressure group. Now I knew her Achilles' heel.

"All I had to do was create some drama. There's no aphrodisiac like drama. At the time, the Nova Scotia elite was becoming interested in the fate of the piping plover. It was endangered because the beaches where they lay their eggs were being taken over by three-wheelers. It took me several weeks to find the right spot.

"One Saturday morning I positioned myself over a plover's egg and started yelling at the three-wheeler fans passing by. To be surer of my results, I brought out the four words of French I remembered. The bikers' reaction was beyond my wildest dreams: a broken arm, a black eye, three fingers twisted—and a paragraph on the front page of the *Halifax Tribune*.

"In my hospital bed, I kept my finger-splints crossed. The day before I was due to be discharged, when I'd given up hope, I heard a familiar voice in the corridor: it was Margie, coming to comfort the environmental champion.

"Our meeting was trite, more like an exchange of vital statistics. She was more impressed by my hero status than by me personally. I'd found the chink in the armour of the virtuous spouse who was once my partner in cannabis.

"That chink was her virtue itself. Margie had a tremendous need to believe in, to belong to her husband and children, to her finer feelings, to God, to the piping plover—you name it. If I wanted to win her over I'd have to become the guardian of her faith. In a word, I'd have to become a saint, of all things!

"As she was leaving, Margie invited me to join her environmental group. Nothing could have made me happier. Here was the perfect spot to practise sainthood! In less than three months I was the piping plover's Father Teresa. I went to every meeting, every demonstration, every press conference. My collar, the sling I kept my arm in weeks after it was healed, my zeal at defending anything that even looked like a nest made me a local hero. At municipal election time there were impassioned debates, with the environmentalists on one side, bikers on the other. All this time was devoted to approach manoeuvres. Margie became my right arm, my bodyguard. She was transformed: she believed.

"After the election, when the plover gained official protection from the Nova Scotia government, I left the environmental group. Exhausted and drained by an inner conflict, I announced that I was giving up political action to devote myself to my ministry.

"This was the crucial step. Had the hook held fast? I took my distance from Margie and put on a show of being bothered by her presence. I went on a diet and lost ten pounds. Wounded by my withdrawal, she regained her faith and started coming to see me at the rectory twice a week. I was more saintly, more sombre than ever.

"One day I asked her, for the salvation of my soul, to stop coming to see me. Beneath her anxiety I sensed that she was radiant: she inspired passion in her confessor! When she was about to leave, in tears, I jumped on her. She put up only token resistance. She was overjoyed at my newfound vigour.

"The rectory became a dangerous place. We got together twice a week at a nearby motel. Using every trick in the book, I applied myself to making her crazy about me. Sex between us was catalysed by a devastating mix of danger, nostalgia, and mysticism. The result was more than I could have hoped for. After two months of this regime, Margie lived only for our meetings. She was neglecting her husband and children, and wasting away before my eyes.

"At first I was flattered, then I developed the

anxiety of the sorcerer's apprentice: I'd lost control over my creation. I was horrified by what sex and religion could cause to grow in a mind left fallow.

"Margie talked about leaving her husband. I spaced out our meetings and became downright obnoxious. Nothing worked. The more I tried to avoid her, the more she loved me. My trap was too perfect: as I tried to loosen the ties between us, they only tightened.

"Worse: Margie's enthusiasm was contagious. I felt the symptoms of a malignant disease within myself: mood swings, tremendous highs and lows, all related to Margie. I was falling in love.

"I left Sydney suddenly, with no explanation. I landed a position in Grosse-Isle. That was two years ago. I felt secure. The bishop's palace and my family kept quiet about my new posting. I started making monthly visits to my old friend in Halifax. After a year I could go through my mail without being afraid. The adventure in Sydney soon seemed like a nightmare.

"Then I ran into Margie at the Halifax airport this summer. She was working at a travel agency and she'd found my name in the computer. She was standing by the baggage carousel, radiant, holding flowers, sure she'd overcome any resistance on my part.

"I was a wreck. I followed her to a hotel. And there, nothing."

"Nothing?"

"Limp as a jellyfish . . . I was useless. Margie wanted to join me in the Islands. Things had changed. Anglican priests were allowed to marry a divorced woman now.

"She was divorced?"

"About to be. Imagine being married to a woman like Margie. What would people say? Not to mention Him. . . . "

"The husband?"

"No."

The little man pointed a trembling finger towards the ceiling. François peered dreamily at the tongue-in-groove that held up the bed where Charlene had huddled. Crazy. This man was as crazy as. . . .

"You told me you'd become a minister because it was an easy way out. Do you believe in God?"

"I got caught up in the game. When Margie wanted to move in with me, I felt guilty for the first time. I was overcome by doubt: what if everything I'd been saying was true? Now I know: He watches me, He punishes me. Margie just came back into my life to impose one last temptation. I left her in Halifax, threatening all sorts of terrible things if she followed me. And now she's here."

Jeffrey Ballantyne curled up in his chair a little more. Robidoux repressed his urge to laugh. The priest's story had almost made him forget about Charlene's getaway.

"You should leave the church, live like other men," he ventured to suggest.

Father Jeffrey leapt from his chair.

"Do you know what sin is, Doctor?"

"I think so."

"Do you know what it's like to live with the feeling that you've ruined your life, that you're neither a man nor a man of God, just an insignificant louse, an alcoholic laughing-stock? And still believing in spite of everything, and waiting to be punished? And the Zulus, Doctor? Have you given a thought to the Zulus?"

He was haranguing a phantom audience. François gave him a dirty look. How could he have allowed this nut-case to ruin his night with Charlene?

"I HAVEN'T THOUGHT ABOUT THE ZULUS, Father Jeffrey! Now, if you don't mind, I'm going back to sleep."

All at once the little man calmed down and pulled

a flask of gin from his pocket.

"What am I going to do?"

François took a healthy swig.

"Ignore her. Let people think she's crazy."

"She'll tell everybody."

"You aren't the first priest who's been the object of that kind of rumour."

"And my . . . ailment?"

François Robidoux took the priest by the shoulder and walked him to the door.

"Get rid of Margie and everything will work out."

Jeffrey Ballantyne stood in the porch, contrite and tearful. He drained the bottle.

"Forgive me, I'm at my wits' end. I said the Zulus, but I could have said the Maori or the Paduang or even the Australopithecans."

"Even the Australopithecans, that's a fact."

"When they die, where do they go? Limbo, purgatory, or hell?"

"I'd bet purgatory. It's warm there. They'd feel at home."

"You're a sly man, Doctor."

The priest went on his way. François wondered if his story was a drunk's joke. Perhaps men of the cloth spent Hallowe'en on Entry.

He dragged himself up the stairs. It was no dream: the bedroom was empty. He sat on the bed, looking for a note from Charlene, but the only thing he found, abandoned on the chair, was his wallet. She had taken off with his trousers. In a blind rage, he kicked and punched at the air. Then he sat down, devastated. She couldn't help playing a practical joke. He tried to laugh, but all he produced were some discordant sounds.

A greyish light was seeping onto the horizon. He curled himself into a ball around the pillow where she'd lain her head. It smelled of cinnamon and sweat. He closed his eyes. For an hour, images swirled around. Then, as daylight came and pressed against the window, he fell into a dreamless sleep.

Chapter 16
Moon

Panting and shaking with bursts of laughter that are condensed in the autumn night, she runs through the small valley that leads to her father's house, carefully holding in her arms a pair of trousers. The southeast wind, heavy with rain, stirs her hair, where silvery spindrift gleams. Between her thighs, she still feels the chilliness of his sperm. She closes her eyes and runs even faster. The spruce woods. The trees are stunted, chewed by the salt wind, their flesh threatened by hearts carved by generations of children. She skips across the root she guesses at lying in the ditch beside the path. She is flying, she is once again a little island girl, the wind is carrying her, with full sail, supreme.

She stops. Under a branch an opening goes towards the left. In the middle of the three willows, she finds the treehouse that she wrecked one day with her brothers. She reaches out her hand, strokes the hairy trunks. Children have moved the ladder and fabricated a roof from a piece of the cabin of a boat. She climbs up, and there in the branches she discovers the sea and Devil's Cape. She sits in a damp chair whose springs nip her buttocks. Hugging the trousers again, she laughs. She listens to the waves breaking against the cliff. Carefully, she rolls up the trousers and buries them in her childhood hiding-place.

She shudders. Then jumps down from her perch

and races back towards the house. As she is leaving the
woods, a hand grabs her wrist.

Chapter 17
A Few Pieces of Pink Sandstone

"Doctor! Doctor!"

Mrs. Patterson was calling from the bottom of the stairs. She stood there, distraught, frozen in a tragic pose.

"Charlene Collins. . . . She's been found at the bottom of the cliff."

"What's she doing there?"

"She's DEAD! Dead, understand? Follow me."

François Robidoux emerged brutally from the night. Charlene was dead. Pain shot through him.

"What happened? An accident?"

"I don't know. She must have fallen off the cliff."

He went back to the bedroom and felt a chill down his spine.

His pants! What was he going to do? Charlene found dead at the bottom of the cliff. What had she done with his pants?

He took off his bathrobe, then donned it again.

"There's a problem, Mrs. Patterson!"

"What problem, for Christ's sake?" the nurse shouted as she swept up the stairs.

"I haven't got my trousers."

She glared at him, furious.

"I tore them."

As a woman who could no longer be surprised by anything, Gladys Patterson merely groaned.

"I'll be right back."

Five minutes later François was wearing the pants from Bill Patterson's wedding suit and he was climbing onto his widow's three-wheeler. An image haunted him: Charlene, with a lock of hair across her cheek, was smiling at him as he left the bedroom to open the door for Father Jeffrey. The rain lashed at their faces. From the lighthouse came the foghorn's mournful call.

The dirt road was transformed into a path that snaked between the hillocks. A dozen bystanders were crowded at the edge of the cliff. The men were busily setting up ropes. Standing out of the way, a couple of women were talking *sotto voce*. François Robidoux tried to think. If his pants had been found near Charlene, he'd have some explaining to do.

"Who found her?" asked François as they were walking towards the group.

"Borden Welsh says he spotted her this morning when he was hunting geese."

Borden Welsh. His truck had been parked near the harbour when François went to meet Charlene. Had he noticed him?

"Any clues?"

"I couldn't say. He was too upset to say anything, really."

Devil's Cape was a rocky promontory that dominated the east coast of the island. All you could see from it was the sea. It was a desolate spot, off the road that Charlene would have taken to go home. What had she been doing there at four a.m.?

She was lying down there on her back, her neck stretched out grotesquely. François Robidoux knew she was dead. People were looking at him strangely.

He went up to the men. One of them was about to go down. Borden's eyes were bulging as he told his story to the group.

"I'll go down first," said François. "If she's alive I may be able to do something."

François suffered from such severe vertigo that he couldn't even climb a ladder. But now he let himself slide down the thirty metres of cliff between him and the young woman. He stood on some rocks that were beleaguered by the waves. There lay Charlene. Just a body like any other, cold and pitiful, that had nothing to do with the laughing creature he had spent the night with. He examined the surroundings, turned the corpse over: not a sign of his pants.

He looked at the body again. It hurt him to look at the open eyes. Closing them, he felt a sudden urge to cry. Charlene's death couldn't be an accident. Who could have killed her? A girl like her didn't commit suicide. On this dirty morning he was waking from a dream in which she'd given him a glimpse of paradise. Despite the brevity of their encounter, despite her stunt with the pants, he felt as if he'd lost the person dearest to him in the world. He had to control himself: if he cried he'd look suspicious. Already an Anglo was at his side, leaning over the broken body. Neither of them spoke. François knew they were both thinking about the old man who was waiting in his chair for them to bring him, wrapped in a blanket, the body of his daughter.

Getting a boat out in weather like this was out of the question. Soon there were six men watching over the corpse. While others were getting a stretcher up above, they moved the body closer to the cliff, to keep it from the tide. Weighed down by their burden, they came to a steep footpath which they were able, with great difficulty, to climb up back to the plateau.

The islanders formed an arc around the dead woman. They had tried unsuccessfully to find Father Jeffrey. There was muttering in the crowd. Preachers:

they're never there when you need them. . . .

"Warren's boat went out before daybreak," said a voice. "Maybe Father Jeffrey went back to Grosse-Isle."

Paler than a cloud, Randy Aitkens went up to the body, touching it to convince himself that it existed. He recovered his senses and gave an order to look for Father Jeffrey. He took the head of the lugubrious procession that stretched out towards the Collins house. François Robidoux, stunned and shivering, walked in the middle of the islanders. No one said a word. All conformed to the ritual, unhesitating, like actors performing for the hundredth time. There had been other deaths. On other mornings, processions had made their way to other houses. It was something known even to the children, who had left their cartoons to flank the column.

Margie Stone came up to the doctor, sniffing.

"What happened to that poor girl?"

"No idea. What are you crying about? You said that death was the big trip. . . . "

"Not like that. Where's Jeffrey? Have you heard from him?"

François shrugged. Don Juan in a cassock was the furthest thing from his mind. What was he going to tell the police?

The Collins house looked tiny against the flank of Big Hill. The windows of the studio cast some light into the greyness. Randy Aitkens went inside, followed by the stretcher-bearers. They left right away, making room for the family. The crowd stayed outside, silent. Then some murmurs rose and the gathering dispersed. Randy and a group of men took Borden Welsh to a nearby house.

François Robidoux and Margie Stone stood in front of the house. They were outsiders. No one was paying any attention to them. Suddenly, Mrs. Patterson appeared and beckoned to the doctor.

"I'm going with you," said Margie Stone.

"Stay there!" ordered Mrs. Patterson. "Pick up your rags and go back where you came from! It'll be better for everybody!"

The nurse headed for the house where the mayor and Borden had gone inside. Only now did François Robidoux notice how she looked. Her eyes were smudged with mascara, her hair tangled, hands shaking.

Mrs. Patterson realized he was looking at her.

"Will you forgive me for yesterday, Doctor? I was drunk."

He was about to say he'd already forgotten the episode when he realized it might wound her.

"Don't think about it."

"I'd love to know what Borden Welsh was doing on the cliff at eight o'clock this morning."

"You told me he was hunting geese."

"Without a rifle?"

Mrs. Patterson strode like a general on campaign.

"In situations like this, does a doctor have any legal authority?"

"I don't think so. I'll have to ask the coroner. For this kind of . . . accident he has to file a report and request an autopsy."

"Be careful what you say."

They went inside. Ten auburn heads turned to look at them. The mayor glanced unhappily at the nurse and went on.

"You spent the night drinking and you were watching for geese, in the middle of a storm, at eight o'clock in the morning. Is that right?"

"That's what I told you!"

Borden Welsh was a sickly-looking man in his fifties. He was suspected of a thousand crimes and valued for his wit. An unemployed bachelor, he roamed the island, on the lookout for a bottle or some comical event. Sitting on a kitchen chair, scared stiff, he was fidgeting while the men looked at him.

"Where did you spend the night? George says you didn't come home."

"I fell asleep in my truck, near the wharf."

"I was at the harbour at three a.m.," said a voice. "Your truck was there but you weren't in side. I checked, I was going to play a trick on you."

"And if you weren't at home or in your truck, where were you?" asked Randy Aitkens.

Borden was sweating like a pig.

"For the last time, Borden, where were you?"

"I was with a woman. . . . "

Borden with a woman! He usually looked for women on Grosse-Isle. He hadn't been seen with one from the island for ten years.

"Who?"

"He was with me."

The voice came from the living room. The mayor's sister-in-law appeared. She must have come in the back door. She was a fat, red-faced woman whose husband fished around Newfoundland. As a teenager she'd gone out with Borden for a few months. Calmly, she held Randy Aitkens's furious gaze.

"Leave Borden alone," she said. "He didn't kill Charlene. He was at my place till dawn. Then he went to the cape for some fresh air. It's his favourite spot. We used to play there when we were children."

There was deathly silence.

"For God's sake, keep your mouths shut," she said, making her way to the door. "When Bruce gets back I'll explain things."

She went out. Prostrate on his chair, Borden Welsh stared at the toes of his boots. François Robidoux was relieved: the man had been with his lady-love while he was waiting on board the *Melinda D*. Randy sighed and asked for a stiff drink of something.

"How was it that you found the body? You'd have had to go to the edge of the cape."

"There were footsteps leading to the edge. I had a funny feeling. So I went up and I found her. I ran over to Gladys's and she sent me to get help. And that's it."

"It may be suicide," someone said. "We didn't know her. She was slightly cracked."

"She must have fallen," said the mayor. "She used to go out at night sometimes and walk along the cliffs."

"How do you know that?"

Randy Aitkens looked down.

The men conferred, reaching a consensus to the effect that it was an accident. Randy had regained his composure.

"I'll go and tell the police."

Some of the men grumbled. They became aware of the doctor's presence and a sense of uneasiness surfaced. Randy Aitkens asked him to be discreet about what Borden had said.

"You can trust me."

François Robidoux headed back for Devil's Cape with Mrs. Patterson. They walked along, each of them deep in thought, battling the east wind that peppered them with icy droplets. At the edge of the cliff he studied the footprints. Marks left by the bystanders had made them impossible to identify. He walked along the hill for three hundred metres, looking for some sign. There was only the sea and the wind coming patiently, wave after wave, gust after gust, to tear chunks of pink sandstone from the cliff. The tide now covered the spot where Charlene had fallen.

Standing to one side, Mrs. Patterson let Robidoux wander. Five minutes later, she shouted his name, very loud to be heard over the wind. François shook himself. They got on the three-wheeler and made their way to the clinic.

A pleasant feeling of warmth greeted them as they walked in the door. Someone had cleaned up, adjusted the temperature, and left some pies in the kitchen.

"Phyllis has been here," said Mrs. Patterson.

François Robidoux went upstairs. The nurse's diary, wedged behind the head of the bed, had escaped Phyllis Dickson's attention. He hid it in a closet, flushed the toilet, and came back downstairs.

Mrs. Patterson was making tea. Silently, François Robidoux went from one window to another.

"Have you got your trousers? I'll mend them."

"I burned them."

He went crimson. Mrs. Patterson said nothing. She poured the tea and went into the examining room, then came out with a yellowing, dog-eared death certificate.

"I think you have to complete this. The police will be here soon."

"You must not use these certificates very often."

"I always keep a couple on hand. When Anna McLean died three years ago, they had to send a boat to Cap-aux-Meules, through the December ice, to bring one back. We couldn't have buried her without it. I had a hard time convincing Dr. Bailly to complete the form over the phone."

The kitchen was a macabre place for this kind of paperwork. François Robidoux wrote the names and dates in the appropriate places. Across the table, Mrs. Patterson read what he'd written. He had checked off "violent death" and asked for a coroner's inquest. His tea was cooling off. He didn't dare look at the nurse.

"You read my diary?"

"Part. You write very well."

"Give it back."

"You lent it to me. I thought we knew each other well enough. It's a fascinating story. Like a novel."

She was beautiful in her disarray. He enjoyed making her languish.

"I was drunk."

"Is your diary that important? I won't tell anyone about it."

"I thought you were more tactful. Would you flaunt your life to a stranger?"

"I'm not a stranger."

"I am. Give me the diary or I'll tell the police about your trousers."

"That doesn't prove anything."

"If they found out that Charlene spent the night here. . . . "

Suddenly he felt like vomiting.

"You were spying on me?"

"My bathroom looks into the clinic. Charlene left here around four o'clock. I don't know what you'd done to her. She was in a big hurry."

"She made off with my pants. Probably a Hallowe'en prank."

"Father Jeffrey came out fifteen minutes later, drunk as a skunk. What a charming trio!"

François Robidoux stood up to collect his thoughts. Mrs. Patterson stayed stiffly beside the table, hands shaking slightly. Suffering from withdrawal, probably.

"What did she do after that?" he asked.

"Ran towards the woods."

"And Jeffrey?"

"He went back to the lighthouse. Did you go to bed with her?"

François Robidoux took out the brandy.

"Why is that diary so important to you?"

"That's got nothing to do with Charlene. It's personal."

"Eva told me you'd poisoned your husband."

He held out her glass. Her lips quivered and she burst into tears.

"Bill died of a cerebral hemorrhage! Eva's been telling everybody I killed him for fifteen years! She's ruined my life!"

"Did you have any reason to kill him?"

"To kill Bill! You're a son of a bitch like the rest of them!"

François Robidoux sat facing the nurse. She went on crying as she drained her glass.

"That poor girl out on the rocks!"

François thought it over. Was it riskier to rely on Mrs. Patterson's discretion than to tell the police? He had a vision of his mother seeing his picture splashed across the front page of the *Journal de Montréal*.

He went upstairs to get the diary and put it on the table in front of him. Mrs. Patterson's hands had stopped shaking.

"Will you be able to hold out during the investigation?"

"I can just say I didn't see anything."

"Do you suspect me? I could have gone out the back door, caught up with Charlene, and killed her."

"Killed her! You don't think it was an accident?"

"Don't you find it strange for a young woman to fall off a cliff in the middle of the night?"

Mrs. Patterson didn't know what to think about

that.

"Father Jeffrey was with you," she began. "You've got an alibi. What did he want?"

"He told me about his affair with the woman on the boat."

"I should have known. You're too kind to push a woman off a cliff."

"Thanks. Have you any idea who did it?"

"It could be Randy Aitkens or any of the men who've been fantasizing about her for three months. Or it could have been suicide."

"Why would you lie for me?"

"I'm in love with you. Don't you know that?"

"I'm not in love with you."

"You don't have to be. Just come and visit and talk to me. I'm a crazy old fool."

François Robidoux was certain she wouldn't betray him. He took a deep breath and slowly, like someone slipping a ring onto his fiancée's finger, pushed the diary towards her. She took his hand and led him to the living-room sofa. He didn't dare to resist.

"Sit down. Like that."

She put her head on his shoulder and curled up against him. She looked like a child exhausted by a tantrum. He stroked her hair absent-mindedly. What was he doing here? His name would be implicated in the story, his career compromised. It was time to re-trace his steps and tell the police the truth. He'd slept with the girl and then she'd run off with his pants—as a prank. Such a story, while unlikely to clear him, would be bound to make him look ridiculous. Father Jeffrey couldn't be a witness. He'd only heard the door close. That left Mrs. Patterson. Curled up in the fetal position, her fist clenched on his shirt, she was the very image of exhaustion. She'd fall apart.

"We have to tell the police everything," he said.

"They'll suspect you. Even accuse you."

"I've got your testimony and Jeffrey's."

"A pair of drunks. The police mustn't know that you slept with Charlene. You'll end up in court. Who knows what can happen during a trial?"

"If they find out the truth I'll be twice as suspect."

"People won't talk. The police have never got to the bottom of anything on Entry Island."

François looked out the window. Never had he imagined rain like this, except in a tropical country. Water was seeping in under the window. He thought about the nurse's diary.

"Time to put on the storms," he said.

"Don't talk about that."

"You should leave now. The police will be here at any moment."

"I won't say a thing about Charlene."

"Yes, it's better that way. Find me some pants that aren't so gaudy."

She tidied her hair. Before she left, with the diary stowed inside her anorak, she kissed the doctor on the lips. Shivering, he shut the door behind her.

Chapter 19
Sergeant Plogueuil

The rain had stopped. The wind continued to lash the jetty with spray. The Coast Guard patrol boat circled the buoy and approached the harbour. A dozen men were following its progress. Like a crowd watching the exit at a roller-coaster, they were anxious to see how the occupants looked.

Pitching and yawing, with an acrid smell of oil escaping from the stern, the boat entered the harbour. Through the hatchway came a sailor's head. He prepared to come alongside with all the majesty of those paid double for overtime. After his red face, those of the passengers left no doubt as to which race they belonged to.

Dr. Pépin appeared, his belly flourishing, suitcase in hand, his manner that of a tourist disembarking onto Everest from a charter flight. Behind him, a young policeman, elegant in uniform, tugged at his blond moustache. He was deep in conversation with a doll-faced thirty-five-year-old, green beneath her make-up. With a tape recorder slung over her shoulder, her right hand clutching the beret that crowned her permanent, she was battling with the wind over her contact lenses.

"Who's that?"

"Radio Canada," said Randy Aitkens.

"Shit!"

Finally, Sergeant Moreau appeared. He seemed to

be suffering the most. Clutching an ancient overcoat to his neck, he crossed the deck, hanging on to the guardrail. With his bulging eyes, cheeks that quivered under the motor's vibration, a big head that threatened to drop at any moment, he looked more than ever like the sea toad to which he owed his nickname, Plogueuil.

He was impatient for the boat to come alongside. Grabbing an outstretched hand, he hoisted himself onto the wharf, ignoring the broadcaster, who was hurrying to his side. Swatting at a tear, she resolutely set one high-heeled boot on the tractor tire flanking the jetty.

Randy Aitkens stepped up to greet the new arrivals.

"Good morning, Sergeant. . . . "

Embarrassed, the mayor realized that he only knew the sergeant by his nickname.

"Moreau, Randy, the name's Moreau. You know the doctor? And this is Officer Matte."

Officer Matte wore a polite, ironic smile. Dr. Pépin was delighted at this adventure.

"This lady's a journalist," said the sergeant.

"I know," said Randy.

He gestured to Winston. Grinning, the deaf-mute took the young woman's tape recorder and led her to a truck. She turned around, furious at being separated from the group. The sergeant looked away.

"A tragic accident . . . ," Randy began.

"Where was the body found?"

The sergeant wasn't here as a tourist. The four men piled into the mayor's jeep.

"Let me hear your version of the story."

Sergeant Cyril Moreau was an enigma to his superiors in the Sûreté du Québec. After a brilliant start to his career, the young sergeant had been transferred to the Îles-de-la-Madeleine. Three years later, he'd asked to be exempted from transfers. His superiors had been reluctant. It was unusual to let policemen settle in outlying regions. They fraternized with the locals and lost their effectiveness. Sergeant Plogueuil's statistics, however, demonstrated the contrary. He was accorded first one dispensation, then another. Later, he turned down promotions to stay on the Islands.

A bachelor, he had just one passion that anyone knew about: cards. There were those who suspected that he'd only stayed here to defend, year after year, the title of Magdalen Tarot League champion. Everyone but his subordinates knew that he gambled his paycheques at poker, usually with fraud artists he was trying to nab. Even though he stayed faithful to his '76 Monte-Carlo and bought his clothes at People's, his bank account was the object of the most extravagant suppositions. He was thought to be both federalist and homosexual. His conquests—few but female—gave the lie to half of that rumour.

The sergeant was a nice guy. He'd call fathers to let them know who their daughters were hanging out with, discreetly warn poachers when the game wardens got suspicious. In exchange, he expected the locals not to exceed a reasonable limit. On other matters—drugs, highway safety—his rigour turned out to be exemplary. This mixture of leniency and severity suited the population. At first they'd called him Sergeant Codface, but it was under the name Plogueuil that they finally adopted him.

Randy Aitkens summed up the events. Borden Welsh had found the body of Charlene Collins at the foot of Devil's Cape at eight a.m. She had gone to bed at midnight, at her father's house, and hadn't been seen subsequently.

"But it was Friday night."

"Old man Collins didn't even hear her go out. She was probably walking along the cliff and fell."

"Any reasons for suicide?"

"Maybe. She arrived here from Toronto this summer. Apparently she had a boyfriend there. A strange girl."

"Beautiful too, so they say."

"Not bad."

"No boyfriends here?"

"She kept her distance."

"Nobody's left the island?"

"No sign of Father Jeffrey. Looks like he went out on Warren's boat this morning."

In the back, Officer Matte snickered.

"Can't you see the headline? 'Preacher Murders Young Woman on Hallowe'en!'"

"It was suicide," said Dr. Pépin. "The whole family's always been unstable. Ever see one of Tim Collins's paintings?"

The sergeant's face was green and he gripped the roll bar as he scanned the landscape. There was a chorus of spatters as the jeep left the road and headed for Devil's Cape.

A piece of wood marked the spot where she'd fallen. The elements and the gawkers had wiped out the trail. To set their minds at rest, the policemen spent fifteen minutes splashing around at the edge of the cliff. Waves now covered the spot where the body had been found. When they got back in the vehicle, their feet were soaking.

"Let's take a look at the body," said the sergeant.

"We'll have fun sorting out this one," said Officer Matte. "Those Anglos talk a blue streak."

"Take notes instead of yakking," said the sergeant. "Randy speaks French."

"A bit," Randy acknowledged.

"Do you think it was suicide?" asked Pépin.

"We can't hide anything from you."

"Why?"

Plogueuil didn't answer. Officer Matte plucked at Pépin's sleeve and gestured towards the mayor.

The doctor nodded.

"Suicide. . . . We haven't heard the end of it. But I just remembered something: François Robidoux spent the night here. Let's go to the clinic, Randy."

Chapter 20
Spermatozoa

François Robidoux watched Mrs. Patterson walk away, pensive. Her head was down and she leaned into the wind that was sending the raindrops against her parka with a muffled sound as she started her three-wheeler. She'd never hold up.

It was too late now to retrace his steps. He wandered through the house, hands in his pockets, a Sunday glumness in his heart. He saw again the massive church on which elm trees used to project their moving shadows so long ago. He'd slip away right after the *Introit* to go behind a hedge and read. And so the melancholy afternoon would pass. François would practise his *He shoots, he scores!* in the yard while the adults were inside talking. When he came in, his cheeks aflame, the conversation would end abruptly. Who were they talking about? Madame Tranchemontagne, a mythical character situated somewhere between the goddess Athena and the legendary Quebec music-hall star Alys Robi. According to the mystery surrounding her, the lady lived a highly reprehensible life. With his tie askew, François would survive their comments on his height and his grades, then he'd run to the TV set.

He went into his consulting room and took Charlene's file from the cabinet. Her name was on the upper right corner, over her father's first name and her own date of birth. July 6, 1957. She was twenty-nine. He saw Mrs. Patterson's first note: pneumonia at the age of one. *One-year-old child. Cough and temp. 104 for two days. Penicillin intramuscular. Parents unconcerned.*

In 1967, three ear infections: *Brought in by mother for insomnia. Child sad and impressionable. Family problems. Moving shortly to Toronto. Suggest they see a psychologist there.*

These too-brief notes contrasted with Mrs. Patterson's usual style. At adolescence, François Robidoux found nothing but prescriptions for contraceptives. No other sign of what Charlene Collins had been.

He reread the note from 1967. Maybe she had committed suicide after all. Weird, though, her getting into her father's doctor's bed. Not to mention her running away with his pants. He reviewed the scenes from the night before: a look, the silver necklace in the moonlight, the rolling of Charlene's hips, her sighs, her cries. Now he had only shattered fragments that time would steal from him, one by one. Already her living face was becoming cloudy in his memory. What he saw at this moment was the face at Devil's Cape, the head thrown back, the staring eyes. He had made love to a dead woman.

Now pain was gnawing at his stomach. Death was on the prowl. He paced the house, his eyes filled with tears. He was afraid. Charlene hadn't killed herself. There was a murderer on the island. His pants hadn't vanished into thin air. They had disappeared between the clinic and the cliff. He tried to slow his breathing.

"Have to keep calm," he said aloud.

The sound of his voice reassured him.

"First, get rid of any trace of her."

He went upstairs to the bedroom. The pillows still smelled of cinnamon. He breathed it in, then sprayed them with an air freshener he found in the bathroom. He carefully gathered up all the long hairs, left the short ones, looked under the bed, inside the closet, up and down the stairs and in the hall, then he got under the shower.

That left Bill Patterson's pants. He pulled them on and saw nothing comic about the situation. On this November first morning, he found himself cruelly lacking any sense of humour. He could only hope that Mrs. Patterson would remember to bring another pair of pants.

He forced himself to eat something. He was going to have to confront the police. They were shrewder than people thought. His hands would give him away. Gigi Bengale had told him he was a coward. "If you want to be a great doctor, why not go to the States or France or one of the big medical faculties?" And Charlene: "You're scared. You just stand there like an intruder and wait."

Freud must be frantic back at the house. He called his friend Jolicoeur.

"What's all this about a suicide?" asked the coordinator. "Is it your Anglo girlfriend or what?"

"Don't be a smartass, okay? Have you seen Freud?"

"He's fine. Hardly noticed you aren't here. What happened? Did Timmy Collins's daughter really jump off a cliff?"

"I'll tell you about it tonight."

Speaking French made him feel better. A motor rumbled outside. André Pépin knocked at the clinic door.

"What's the matter with you? Your face is as long as Lent. Did you spend the night on the clothesline? Come on, we're going to examine the body."

"I'm glad to see you."

"What's that you're wearing? You look like an undertaker."

"My pants got soaked at the cliff this morning. Mrs.

Patterson lent me these. They were her husband's."

Bill Patterson's trousers were definitely not discreet. Looking more dead than alive, François Robidoux ran out to the jeep with his colleague. Plogueuil shook hands, then returned to his meditations. Beside him, the officer was scribbling something on a steel clipboard.

There were still enough Collinses on Entry Island to fill the ground floor of a small house. The women were in the kitchen, the men in the living room. When the doctors and policemen arrived, they all fell silent. Sergeant Plogueuil went around shaking hands.

Charlene had been laid out on her bed, in what used to be her parents' bedroom. The sergeant examined the body. From his case, Pépin took a microscope, slides and bottles, a pathologist's kit that fascinated Officer Matte.

Dr. Pépin approached the body.

"A terrible shame. She was a lovely girl. Looks like her head was smashed against a rock."

"Or else somebody did it for her," said the sergeant.

François Robidoux stood discreetly off to the side. The other doctor and the sergeant undressed the corpse and dropped the clothes into a plastic bag. Soon the body was naked, snow white in the wood-panelled room. The sea had washed the skin, tangled weeds in the hair, deposited sand in the corners of the eyes. The right cheek and temple were swollen. At the top of the thighs, the pelvic bones widened into a useless temple. The fingers were bare of rings. François was surprised to see traces of mauve polish on the toenails. He wouldn't have thought Charlene capable of such a thing.

All they could hear was the creaking of Officer Matte's pen.

"Look, Sergeant, a mark on the neck. . . . "

Above the right clavicle, François Robidoux saw a threadlike abrasion three centimetres long. The necklace had disappeared.

"Strangled?" asked Matte.

"I don't think so," said Pépin. "It's just on one side."

Sergeant Plogueuil groaned.

"We'll leave that to the pathologist. Let's go call on Timmy Collins. We're forgetting our manners."

He and the officer went out. François Robidoux was left there alone with Pépin, who took out two pipettes and set up his microscope.

"Any ideas?" asked Pépin.

"Not one. We saw Timmy Collins yesterday. Charlene seemed sad. But I'd never have thought she'd do a thing like this."

"You think she killed herself?"

"I never understood what she was doing on Entry Island. She had a good job in Toronto, a boyfriend. She left all that behind to come here."

"She wasn't the first one to do that. They miss their island."

"Maybe she was depressed."

"Not for lack of company. Take a look."

François Robidoux bent over the microscope. Some of his own sperm were swimming frenziedly before his eyes.

"Still alive and kicking," said Pépin. "It's only been a few hours."

"Maybe she was raped."

Pépin dropped part of the sample into a sealed bottle. Since the examination began he'd been impressively serious. François Robidoux searched his memory: could an individual be identified by his sperm? He walked to the window, scrawled his initials in the condensation.

"Lousy weather."

"This directs our investigation," said Pépin. "It limits the possibilities."

Sergeant Plogueuil and Officer Matte left the bedroom. The family had gone, as had Randy Aitkens. A lady of indeterminate age was playing solitaire at the kitchen table.

"Is Mr. Collins here?"

She jerked her head in the direction of the staircase.

"Find Father Jeffrey," Plogueuil ordered the officer. "Call the airport, the ferry, Grosse-Isle, everywhere."

"If we had a German shepherd we could just let him sniff a bottle."

The sergeant went upstairs. Slumped in his chair, Timothy Collins was spreading red paint onto a blank canvas. Very soft piano music filled the studio.

The policeman cleared his throat.

"Take a seat, Sergeant."

Collins was breathing noisily. Merely moving his left hand seemed to exhaust him. He was painting with the feverishness of a man searching for his passport in a messy room.

He put down his brush.

"This is no good."

Ignoring the policeman, he studied his canvas.

"It's shit."

"Sorry to disturb you today. . . . "

"Ask your questions."

He and Charlene had eaten supper around seven o'clock, after Mrs. Patterson and Dr. Robidoux had left. She'd stayed in to greet the trick-or-treaters. Around ten, she'd gone upstairs and they'd listened to music together. She said something about going to the Community Hall, then changed her mind and went to bed early, around eleven.

"You didn't hear her go out last night?"

"No."

"You didn't hear anything?"

"No."

"Do you take sleeping pills?"

"No, goddammit, I don't take drugs."

"When did you fall asleep?"

"Around one."

"So Charlene snuck out during the night."

"You're the detective."

"Why would a young woman sneak out in the middle of the night?"

"To see a man. Usually."

"Dr. Robidoux?"

The painter guffawed.

"She thought he was pretentious."

"Who, then?"

"No idea. Charlene could go out at night to look at the sea from the cliffs. She went in for that kind of thing."

"Would you call her frivolous?"

"Call it what you want."

"Could she have killed herself?"

"Never. She was happy since she'd come back here. Somebody killed her. Look around the island, you'll find out who."

"You suspect someone."

"Nothing precise. But I know she was killed."

"Did she have enemies?"

"She was beautiful and happy. That's enough."

Sergeant Plogueuil walked to the window. The sun's rays pierced the clouds and cast a yellow beam onto the sea. The crests of the waves glittered under the cope of humidity that hung over the archipelago. The wind grew calmer, then resumed its furtive course.

"Did she wear any jewellery?"

"Rarely."

"There's a mark on her neck. The murderer tried to strangle her, or else ripped off a necklace."

The painter went pale and fell silent. His thoughts were wrapped around a memory or a musical phrase. Plogueuil made a gesture of irritation.

"Will you authorize us to search the house and do a post-mortem?"

"Do whatever you want, with her body and anything else. I don't want any memories of her dead. I've told you everything I know. What goes on outside this studio interests me less and less."

"Even Charlene's death?"

"What I think about that is none of your business, Sergeant. Do what you can with the facts."

Plogueuil looked at the canvas, where the red was turning dull as it dried.

"Is that for her?"

"It's not for anybody. I don't think I'll paint any more."

"You can't just stop. Life's like that."

"What do you know about it?"

Plogueuil rose, savouring in his turn the pleasure of leaving a question unanswered. Bidding Collins goodbye, he left the room.

On the phone downstairs, Officer Matte was trying, in the version of English he'd picked up in rural Quebec, to get information from an obtuse listener. Sighing, Plogueuil looked out the kitchen window. The gap in the clouds had closed in.

"Could we have some coffee, ma'am?"

The card-player gestured towards the stove and slapped a jack of spades onto a queen of hearts. All that Plogueuil could see was an iron pot in which four teabags had boiled.

"Coffee?"

The woman pointed to the cupboard. Plogueuil gave up and went to the bedroom. Charlene's body had been turned on one side. Pépin was examining the back and the nape of the neck. Meanwhile François Robidoux, even whiter than the dead woman, was opening the pine armoire that contained her clothes.

"Don't touch anything, Dr. Robidoux," said Plogueuil. "I'd like to ask you a few questions."

Uncomfortable, the young doctor followed him to the living room. François Robidoux recounted October 31—his visit to the Collins house, supper with Mrs. Patterson, his meeting with Margie Stone, and his return to the clinic. He passed over his trip to the port and Charlene's visit.

"You went to bed early? You seem tired."

"Jeffrey Ballantyne came to the clinic at four a.m. He had a stomach ache."

"He came to the clinic in the middle of the night for a stomach ache! He must have been in terrible pain."

"He was drunk. He told me about some other matters, but I'm bound by professional secrecy."

"I see. Would these other matters be useful to the investigation?"

"I can't talk about them. I'm sure you understand my position."

Robidoux was thinking fast. The clergyman's visit and his disappearance were providential. They diverted suspicions and established his professional credibility by forcing him to respect a patient's confidence.

Margie Stone would be only too happy to talk about her relationship with Jeffrey. He wouldn't even have to mention it.

"Did Ballantyne keep you up very long?"

"An hour or so."

"So it was five o'clock when he left?"

"I didn't look at the time."

"Then what?"

"I went to bed but I couldn't sleep. Mrs. Patterson told me about Charlene at eight o'clock. You know the rest."

"Did you know Charlene Collins very well?"

"She used to call me often about her father."

"Did you like her?"

"I didn't have the nerve to tell her. She intimidated me."

"Why?"

"She had a way of looking down on you. She was very close to her father. When you were around her, you could feel yourself being compared with him."

"You can go now. I'll call if I need you. Are you going back to Cap-aux-Meules today?"

"I'd like to."

Voices rose from the porch. Under the mayor's direction, two men were manoeuvring a narrow coffin. The fresh aroma of pine filled the room.

François Robidoux let them pass, then went out. Officer Matte put down the phone.

"Our man took the plane to Halifax this morning. He bought his ticket at the counter. The girl at Air Canada said he looked like a guy coming home from the lobster festival."

"That's how he usually looks. Advise the Halifax people. What's the population of the island, Randy?"

"One hundred and sixty-seven."

"Make a list of everyone who was on the island last

night, and their ages."

"Including women and children?"

"I'll sort them out."

In the bedroom, Dr. Pépin was putting away his material.

"She had sexual relations in the past twenty-four hours."

"Interesting. Any marks on the body?"

"Some on the left half of the skull. They could be from the fall. The pathologist will sort that out better than I can."

They wrapped Charlene Collins' body in a blanket and laid it in the temporary coffin. One of the men took out a hammer. The blows rang out through the house. Sergeant Plogueuil thought of Timmy Collins. Say what you want, there are advantages to being an old bachelor.

Chapter 22
Ramshackle Armour

Mrs. Patterson stepped out of the shower. She avoided looking in the mirror. The sight of her flaccid breasts, of the stretch marks striating her belly, of the grey hairs that haunted her pubis, was unbearable to her. She wrapped herself in a bathrobe and sat at her mirror.

Her face bore the patina of the years. Where her cheeks had once curved inwards, now they fell straight to the jaw and past it, leaving under the bone that was once so fine a dividing line of fat. Under a microscopic bombardment, the gaunt chin had become a lattice-work of craters that appeared as soon as she opened her mouth. The hairs that had sprouted beneath her nose spelled menopause. Only her eyes still had their sparkle. Slightly moist, the whites mapped with small veins, they blazed out from a web of wrinkles, glorious, two crusaders returning home in their ramshackle armour.

She sipped some brandy. She touched up her cheeks, drew a pencil line around her eyes, gathered her hair into a fur hat. Gladys Hadfield had vanished. She was looking now at Mrs. Patterson, the Entry Island nurse on whom Radio-Canada had done such a fine story three years ago.

He had no more power over that woman.

Chapter 23
Highlights

While he'd expected to find some fog in the islanders' depositions, Sergeant Plogueuil had miscalculated its density. Clues dissolved in the ambient dampness. Now and then a shower fell from the sky, like a theatre curtain dropping because of a stagehand's negligence. One whole act was missing from the play that had been put on the night before: everything that had occurred between one o'clock and eight o'clock a.m. It was strange that on this Hallowe'en Friday the entire island should have been quietly sleeping. The islanders had melted the night into a ball whose very smoothness was suspect.

He searched Charlene's room. Nothing of note. The coffin was loaded onto a covered truck. Once again Dr. Pépin and the two policemen piled into Randy's jeep. Leaving Timothy Collins in the care of the card-player, the convoy made its way to Phyllis Dickson's house.

Churchill, his muzzle between his paws, was solemnly meditating. His perpetual station outside the front door was undermining his *joie de vivre*. Phyllis stepped over him thirty times a day, without thinking, even when he'd gone to pee against the corner of the shed.

In the dining room, Radio-Canada and Margie Stone gazed at the new arrivals, their eyes bright with a brand-new complicity. They were surfacing from a long conversation.

"I thought you'd forgotten all about me, Sergeant," said Radio-Canada.

"I'll be making a statement this afternoon. It's up to you to get your information."

"That's what I intend to do."

The journalist slipped on her coat.

"It's starting to rain again. Would you like Winston to guide you?"

"He's not very talkative. Thanks anyway."

In the driving rain, Radio-Canada left on her assignment.

"Her colour's going to wash away," said Officer Matte.

"Or she'll come down with pneumonia," said Pépin.

"Some truck will pick her up," said Plogueuil. "Ms. Stone? My colleague wants to ask you a few questions."

Red with pleasure, Officer Matte led Margie Stone into the next room. Plogueuil went to the kitchen to ask for coffee. Phyllis Dickson beckoned him closer.

Whenever he came to the island, the sergeant always dropped in to see the widow. Between the sugar and the milk, she would pour out valuable information, with a feigned innocence that delighted them both.

That day, she was more excited than usual.

"Did you know that Randy was in love with Charlene?" she whispered. "It all started when they were children. Ever since she came back he's been different."

"Do you think he killed her?"

She shrugged. The Sergeant sipped his coffee without a word. The Dicksons and the Aitkens, as everybody knew, weren't particularly fond of each other. Randy had been one of the first to take issue with

Phyllis's husband.

Randy and Dr. Pépin came into the kitchen, drawn there by the aroma of coffee. Plogueuil asked the young mayor to summon Borden Welsh and Mrs. Patterson.

Shortly after that the nurse's '69 Ford pulled up behind the house.

"The Old Queen's brought her truck," said Randy.

"The Old Queen?" asked Plogueuil.

"When Gladys was young," said Phyllis, "she was the prettiest woman on the island."

Mrs. Patterson appeared, dressed to kill, looking Victorian with her chignon and rouged cheeks. The sergeant showed her into the dining room.

She'd gone to bed after François Robidoux's departure. Borden Welsh had burst into her place that morning.

"No calls?"

"No."

"The preacher came to the clinic at four a.m., to see the doctor. He should have called you first, shouldn't he?"

"He wouldn't dare wake me up at that hour."

"You aren't on good terms?"

"He knows what I think of him."

"What about Ms. Stone? What's she doing here?"

"She claims she's the priest's mistress."

"Really?"

"It's not surprising."

"Did Charlene have a boyfriend?"

"There isn't a man on this island who didn't dream about going to bed with her."

"Randy?"

Mrs. Patterson hesitated.

"Now that you mention it, I remember that twenty years ago he went berserk over her. When she left at the end of the summer he talked about killing himself. But

I don't know if he's even spoken to her since she came back."

"He's not married, right?"

"You're on the wrong track. Randy would never do a thing like that."

"Last question. Does Mr. Collins take any drugs?"

"Very few. Just for his rheumatism."

"Nothing to help him sleep?"

"The doctor prescribed something but he refuses to take it. He's afraid he'll lose his memory."

The sergeant thanked the nurse. In the next room, Officer Matte, his forehead beaded with sweat, was starting the fourth page of Margie Stone's statement.

"It's good to take notes," said Plogueuil. "Anything interesting?"

"This woman claims to know where to find Father Jeffrey."

"In Halifax. At 227 Grafton Street. With his favourite whore."

"This Father Jeffrey sounds like quite a character, Sergeant."

"Call Halifax. If they find him, tell them to send him here today."

"The flight for Halifax has already left."

"They can ask the RCMP, it'll give them something to do."

Margie Stone was following this exchange in French with the candour of an aborigine at Wimbledon. She was thrilled to see them paying so much attention to her Jeffrey.

"You ought to be worried," said Plogueuil. "The minister's behaviour is quite strange."

"I'm living proof that he couldn't kill a fly. The reason he's afraid of me is because he loves me too much. Do you understand?"

"No."

The two policemen went back to the dining room. The sergeant asked Matte and Randy if they'd drawn up the list of islanders.

Borden Welsh made his entrance, awkward and freshly shaved. Any trace of untidiness had disappeared from his person. He looked like a Jehovah's Witness. Plogueuil questioned him for almost an hour. Borden had spent the night playing cards with some friends. The policeman could ask them, they'd confirm it.

"What were you doing on the cliff this morning?"

"Watching for the wild geese."

"Thank you."

He left.

"Randy, since when has Borden Welsh been interested in hunting geese? Can he even hold a rifle?"

"He's always liked birds."

It was past noon. Plogueuil asked Randy Aitkens to come back for them in an hour. Margie Stone was in her room. The sergeant had lunch with Dr. Pépin and Officer Matte. Through the dining-room window, they could see the truck that was transporting the coffin.

"In a word," said the doctor, "she was raped and then murdered."

"A classic case," said Officer Matte.

"I'd bet on the preacher."

"Surely not. Ms. Stone says he can hardly get it up."

"Precisely. What do you think, Sergeant?"

Plogueuil was eating slowly, head bent over his plate, paying no attention to the others.

"You're jumping to conclusions pretty quickly, Doctor. Charlene Collins went out in the middle of the night. The question to ask is, who was she going to meet?"

"You don't think she was raped?"

"I've got my own ideas about that."

Phyllis Dickson came in with the new cordless phone she'd ordered from Sears.

"Halifax."

The sergeant let his subordinate take the call. Matte jabbered a few "Yes sir's," listened for a while, and put down the instrument, triumphant.

"They got him."

Plogueuil raised his eyes to heaven.

"He was with the woman on Grafton Street. They're sending him over by helicopter, they've really cleared the decks for action. You don't know the best. . . . "

The doctor abandoned his dessert.

"He was involved in the corruption of a minor in 1974. It was settled out of court. He's known as an environmental activist. I told you he was a weirdo."

"They don't make preachers like they used to," said the doctor.

"When does he get here?" asked Plogueuil.

"Around two."

"Phyllis! Call Randy. We're going to the lighthouse."

Chapter 24
Deus ex machina

The lighthouse-keeper's door was unlocked. As soon as he went inside, Plogueuil noticed footprints. There was a rustling of paper in the living room and Radio-Canada appeared, sporting black-framed glasses.

"I lost a lens. I had to come in to take out the other one."

"Contact lenses are like drinking," said Officer Matte. "Something not everyone can tolerate."

Sergeant Plogueuil glanced at his protégé, then went into the living room. A notebook lay open on the sofa, next to some press clippings.

"You like to read?"

"Umm, yes. . . . "

"Detective stories?"

"Sometimes."

"You know that what you're doing is illegal? Just because we're on an isolated island, it doesn't give you permission to stick your nose where it doesn't belong the day after a murder."

"Has there been a murder?"

Sighing, the sergeant studied the clippings. There was a photo of Father Jeffrey Ballantyne, his arm in a sling, demonstrating outside a government office in Halifax.

"Our hero takes care of his legend. Did you find anything else?"

"This."

The young woman shifted a pile of encyclopedias and showed him some pornographic magazines. Dr. Pépin approached.

"These are old issues. The former lighthouse-keeper went in for this kind of literature."

"There's something else," said Radio-Canada.

She took a package from a kitchen cupboard. From it the sergeant removed a vibrator, still sealed in its original wrapping.

The journalist's cheeks flushed discreetly.

"The receipt's inside. Bought in Halifax last month."

"Do you know how they work?" the officer asked the journalist.

"Mario," said Plogueuil.

"Your name's Mario?" asked the doctor. "Mario Matte?"

"We don't get to choose our own names. Sergeant, I told you this priest was a weird one."

Sergeant Plogueuil peered curiously at the vibrator, then handed it to his subordinate.

"Get rid of this. Madame, I have to ask you to leave the house and stick to being a journalist."

Sheepishly, Radio-Canada slipped away. The policemen looked around the house. In a garbage can Plogueuil found the charred remains of a Bible. An open bottle of gin sat on a bedside table. In the closet, two clerical suits reeked of mothballs, while a statement in a drawer testified to the precarious state of the Grosse-Isle parish finances. The priest seemed to have left in a hurry.

A rumbling filled the room. The three men got into Randy's jeep and headed for the airport. From every corner of the island, trucks were converging towards the landing strip. The helicopter hovered, crushing some puddles and brownish grass, then it touched down across from the hangar.

Jeffrey Ballantyne appeared, gaunt and shivering, flanked by two scholarly-looking types in dark glasses. Safe in their trucks, some twenty islanders turned inexpressive faces towards him. The sergeant exchanged a few words with the Nova Scotians. The two policemen gave him an envelope and boarded the aircraft again, which immediately rose into the air, snatched up by the sky, and headed south.

Jeffrey Ballantyne looked first at Plogueuil, then at Officer Matte.

"Are you from the police? Why did you have me brought here like a criminal?"

"You don't know?" asked the officer.

"Is it a crime to protect yourself from a lunatic?"

"Charlene Collins was found dead this morning," said Plogueuil.

He observed the clergyman's reaction. His face showed first surprise, then incomprehension. He launched into a vehement protest and threatened to bring proceedings against the police for slander.

They went back to Phyllis's house to question him. After Margie Stone's visit, he had gone walking on the cliffs to put his thoughts in order, then come back. At about four o'clock, unable to turn the question around any more, he'd gone to the clinic to see Dr. Robidoux.

"How did he receive you?"

"He seemed distracted. At first he didn't want to listen to me."

"What did you talk about?"

"About my relationship with Ms. Stone. I'm sure you know about it. At one point I heard a sound like a door closing. The doctor went white."

"Someone came in?"

"I don't know. I didn't pay much attention."

"What did you do after you left the clinic?"

"Went back to the lighthouse."

"Did you see anybody?"

"Just a truck going towards the hill."

"Could you tell whose it was?"

"It was Randy's."

"Are you sure?"

"Yes."

"And after that?"

"I decided to leave the island."

"Because of Ms. Stone?"

"As a minister of God, it's impossible for me to tolerate her near me."

"What were you going to do?"

"Tell my superiors everything and ask to be transferred out west or to the Zulus."

The sergeant asked the minister to stay at Phyllis's house, where they could reach him.

"If it's all right with you, I'd rather go back to the lighthouse. You understand?" he added, looking up at the ceiling.

Plogueuil gave him permission to leave, then asked Officer Matte to come in.

"Go to the clinic. Search the house inside and out. Charlene may have been there."

The officer left. Dr. Pépin looked at Winston's gums.

"You have to do something about that, Winston. It could cause trouble. Wait, Mario, I'll come with you."

Plogueuil told Randy Aitkens to come in. The young mayor gave him the list of the island's inhabitants. When the policeman asked him about his late-night drive, Randy's lips began to quiver.

"I couldn't sleep. I drove past Charlene's."

"Were you thinking about her?"

"I knew you'd find out I was in love with her. When I told you about my drive last night I was afraid I'd come under suspicion."

"Did you see anything at the Collins house?"

"There was a light on in Timmy's studio. He often gets up very early."

"What time was it?"

"Close to five."

"And Charlene?"

"I didn't see her. I didn't hang around. I went right home."

"It's a dangerous game you're playing, Randy."

"Nobody thought you'd do a serious investigation."

"That's all you've got to tell me? You didn't see Charlene last night?"

"No. I didn't even know she'd gone out. I didn't kill her, Sergeant. I loved her so much. How could I do such a hideous thing?"

He burst into tears. Margie Stone, who had just come downstairs, sidled up to him. Annoyed, the sergeant went to the kitchen for a coffee. Phyllis had left. When he returned to the living room, Margie Stone was talking softly to the young man. Winston was burning shingles in the stove and glancing furtively at them.

Plogueuil went into the dining room and shut the door. The tide of oblivion was receding. Last night's events were rising to the surface. He read the Halifax police report. They had picked up the minister at noon, at 227 Grafton Street. He had put up no resistance. Born in Dartmouth to a Scottish father and an Acadian mother. Identified during a demonstration at the university in 1967. Suspected of cannabis dealing in 1969. Accused of corrupting a minor in 1974, while at the seminary; the complaint had been withdrawn. Following a campaign for the defence of the piping plover, he'd become involved in the last municipal election in Sydney.

A rectangle of light could be seen on the table. In the west, the sun was carving out an opening below the clouds. The rain had stopped an hour ago and the wind was dropping. There were still some details to be clarified.

Chapter 25
Requiem aeternam

Stretched out in the creaking bed, François Robidoux let the sumptuous melancholy of the *Requiem* by his pal Amadeus pour over him. The basses rolled along the tonic notes and fifth notes, suggesting footsteps (the gliding of slippers?) behind a funeral procession. One flat, D minor, four beats, one and two and three and four. When he was a nine-year-old taking his first music lessons, he'd asked the teacher if he could borrow a book about harmony. One week later he could explain keys, rhythms, metrics. Unfortunately, he played very badly. Under his touch the most banal minuet became unbearably mechanical. Listen carefully, François: One and two and three and four and. . . . His internal clock was broken down. Between himself and the music there was a veil. He tore it apart but the veil only grew more opaque. He'd gone back to hockey.

Requiem aeternam. . . .

November 1791. Mozart is strolling through Vienna. The first snow settles on the toy that he's bringing back to the house. He meets a young girl, her face buried in her cape. He turns around, runs to catch up with her. Charlene, with a gaping wound in her cheek, is racing away as fast as her feet will carry her. Mozart returns to his lodgings. He plays with his son and goes back, shuddering, to his scores. Three knocks at the door.

Et lux perpetua. . . .

Officer Matte was pounding on the doorjamb. François Robidoux took off his earphones.

"Mind if we take a look?"

Dr. Pépin appeared and said:

"You didn't go to Phyllis's for lunch? You'll miss the whole investigation!"

"This isn't an Agatha Christie novel," said Officer Matte. "Dr. Robidoux will wait in the living room while I search the house."

"Surely you don't suspect Dr. Robidoux?"

"I'm following orders."

The two doctors went downstairs to the ground floor.

"Young policemen are like doctors fresh out of medical school," said Pépin. "They come to the Islands to practise."

François tried to laugh as naturally as he could.

"A brandy?"

"Excellent idea," said Pépin. "You aren't mixed up in this business, I hope?"

"They're searching the house because of Jeffrey Ballantyne. Was he the one who arrived in the helicopter just now?"

Then François Robidoux inquired discreetly about how the investigation was going. The brandy's sting reminded him of his union with Mrs. Patterson, and comforted him. Above the heads of the two colleagues, the hundred-year-old floor creaked under the footsteps of Officer Matte, who was taking his time in the bathroom. François Robidoux turned white when he thought he heard, twice, the hiss of a room deodorant.

The policeman came downstairs to continue his inspection.

"Nothing interesting?" asked Robidoux.

The officer didn't reply. Pépin looked at Robidoux

and chortled.

"Have you found the murder weapon, Mario? It's clearing up. Let's go out and get some fresh air."

Smiling smugly, Officer Matte went outside with the two doctors. A faint wind from the southwest brought odours of the churning sea from the coast. The windows of the clinic were covered with a fine coating of salt. The hay shimmered, iridescent, in the setting sun. They walked two hundred metres to the cliff. On their left rose Devil's Cape, solitary and indifferent to the comments of the gulls. The bystanders had scattered and the cliff had regained its mineral peace. The image of Charlene dead made Robidoux shudder.

Officer Matte inspected the area around the clinic. He examined the back door, rummaged around in the yard, then headed for the bare forest that separated the clinic from the hill and the Collins house. A path indicated a shortcut. The officer peered for a long time at some footprints.

"Can't see a thing. There're needles all over the place."

François Robidoux looked at the trees. Charlene must have come this way after she left the clinic. He imagined her running, laughing as she clutched his trousers.

On their left, among three big willow trees, they could glimpse a child's treehouse. They emerged into a meadow that flanked the road leading to the Collins house. Five trucks were parked outside it.

They retraced their steps. Mrs. Patterson's venerable pickup truck was perched on a hill near the clinic, its rear end in the air.

They went inside. The nurse was consulting a file in the office.

"My sister-in-law called," she said. "Eva is dying."

All day, François Robidoux had been worried about

his accomplice's silence. Why had she not got in touch with him? Why hadn't she brought him another pair of pants? He'd spent hours imagining the worst scenarios. He realized that his seclusion might seem surprising, but he didn't feel up to confronting the sergeant.

"We're going back to Phyllis's house," said Officer Matte. "We'll have to leave soon if we want to cross while it's still light."

"Coming along?" asked Pépin.

"I'll join you after my house call."

The two men left.

"They suspect something, don't they?" asked Mrs. Patterson.

"I told you it wouldn't work. They'll find out that Charlene was here. I should have told them right away."

Mrs. Patterson didn't reply. Holding Charlene's open file, she was listening to something. François Robidoux pricked up his ears. All he heard was the sound of the jeep driving down towards the harbour.

"What's the matter?" he asked.

"Nothing."

She had aged ten years since last night.

"Did you think about me?" he asked.

"Here's an old pair of Thomas's pants. They should fit. Stop worrying. You'll only look suspicious."

They drove to Eva Patton's house. The seats in the pickup were comfortable. François rolled down his window and breathed in the cold air. Mrs. Patterson was right. The police had no serious reason to suspect him. The island was a small place. The murderer had to be somewhere. The truth would out in the end.

They spied Radio-Canada going back to Phyllis's, looking numb with cold. François waved to Winston. Churchill barked. In two hours he'd be back with Freud and his house on the Martinique beach. The bad dream would fade away.

At the Pattersons', the daughter-in-law was polishing the stove. She insisted that everything be spotlessly clean for the death of her mother-in-law. Eva Patton was lying in a nest of lace pillowcases, her lips bluish, gurgling from pulmonary edema. Her sheets were clean, her nightgown spotless, her temples cooled with lemon water. In spite of all this she smelled of urine and sweat.

They were alone.

"Mrs. Patton?"

A glimmer of awareness showed in the glaucous eyes. Stimulated by a lack of oxygen, her nerve centres were forcing her to pull like an animal on lungs saturated with water. There was only room in her now for a combat she was doomed to lose.

"Goddamn life! It's worse than a dog. Impossible to get rid of it."

Between François Robidoux's ribs his heart beat like the drum on a slave ship. He was only an obscene spectator now.

"Are you in pain?"

"Tell me what happened last night. I can hear them whispering in the kitchen. They think I'm already on the other side."

"Charlene Collins is dead. She jumped off the cliff."

This revelation sent Eva Patton into limbo. For more than a minute she struggled to regain her breath. Her eyes opened again but she remained silent, absorbed in some memory.

"Do you want me to give you something?" asked Robidoux.

"No. I don't want to lose this moment."

"Do you want to see Father Jeffrey?"

The old lady smiled. François wiped the saliva

from the corners of her lips.

"The people will be glad. Doctor?"

She took his hand. Her fingers were icy. François Robidoux felt panic overcome him. He was stifling.

"Gladys. . . . She killed Bill and. . . . "

He couldn't take any more. He tore himself from the dying woman's grasp and raced to the kitchen. Three Patterson sons who arrived just then gave him an astonished look. He froze in his tracks. Gladys was sitting in the living room by herself.

"Call Father Jeffrey!" he shouted, as if he were asking for the fire department.

Ted Patterson, a gigantic fisherman with brick-red cheeks, looked at his brothers, dumbfounded.

"Are you sure? She hasn't got long?"

"If you want her to receive the sacraments, get him here before the boat leaves. The police may take him back to Cap-aux-Meules."

The Pattersons hesitated. Did their mother's sins deserve absolution by an alcoholic murder-suspect?

"They've administered them three times," said one brother.

"One time more or less. . . . "

Ted Patterson went out to look for the priest and François retreated to the living room. Mrs. Patterson, her eyes closed, was rocking in a chair. He sat next to her and took his time writing a long note. Slowly, he regained possession of himself. He missed the warmth of the hospital and his work.

He laid down his pen. Father Jeffrey came in. He placed his diminutive hand in each of the fishermen's paws, murmuring sympathy. The silence weighed heavily. No one brought up his escapade in Halifax or the death of Charlene Collins. The family went with him to the dying woman's bedside, with François Robidoux behind them. The clergyman pretended to ignore him,

as if they were in the habit of meeting in such circumstances. The old lady opened one eye and submissively
allowed him to administer the sacraments, dusting off
some image from her past. The odour of gin filled the
room.

When it was over, Eva Patton raised one hand, then
slumped back lethargically. The men exited the room,
leaving their mother in the charge of her daughter-in-
law. François Robidoux hesitated, then followed them.

Sergeant Plogueuil was in the living room with
Mrs. Patterson.

Virgil Aitkens lowers the safety catch on his revolver. Crouching on the rough planks, he scrutinizes the forest. You have to walk stealthily behind these spruce trees. A twig cracks, a branch sways, and he fires twice. The furtive sounds resume ten seconds later, more and more exciting. How many of them are tracking him?

Escape. First of all, save his weapon. With utmost caution, Virgil Aitkens stands on tiptoe and slips his hand into the hole in the tree. He draws it out, horrified. There's something cold inside. He reaches in again. Cloth. From the hole he removes a pair of corduroy trousers, carefully rolled up.

"Hey, you guys, look at this!"

His two enemies burst from the underbrush and make a run for the treehouse. Holding their rifles, they climb the ladder and surround the stronghold.

"You'd better surrender, Captain!"

Virgil Aitkens shows off his find to his cousins.

"That's a pair of pants," says the younger one.

"Maybe there's money in the pockets," observes the older boy. "Give it here."

Virgil Aitkens turns away and jealously holds on to his booty. In the left-hand pocket he discovers a little change, enough for two Crunchie bars. In the back pocket, a sheet of graph paper with three lines of writing thickened by moisture.

"Shit! It's in French. . . . "
Mozart
Brenda: Vérifier Glycémie
Tonomètre
"Who's Mozart?" asks the youngest of the cousins.
"A new group," says the other confidently.
"Let's show Mom," Virgil decides. "Maybe it's got something to do with Charlene Collins."
The children run through the woods and out in the direction of the corner store. Rain drips from the conifers and their running-shoes squelch through the soaking fields.
Outside the store they deliberate on the question of candy. Just as they're about to go inside, they run into Phyllis Dickson. The fat woman gives them a smile, then stares at their war treasure.
"What's that you've got, Virgil?"
"A pair of pants," says the youngest of the cousins.
"Where did you find them? For heaven's sake, give them to me!"
Phyllis Dickson grabs the pants from her nephew, shoves them under her coat, and walks away, grumbling. Now there's no doubt at all in Virgil's mind: their find has something to do with Charlene Collins's death. He toys with the idea of telling the police, but abandons it for fear of reprisals. Pensively, he goes into the store with his two enemies. He'll keep the paper in his desk drawer just in case, like a treasure map he can't decipher. And when he learns that Mozart was an eighteenth-century Austrian composer, he'll have trouble understanding what that has to do with his neighbour Brenda's glycemia.

The fresh air had put some colour into Sergeant Plogueuil's cheeks. He was uncomfortable turning up at the Patterson's under the circumstances. He asked Father Jeffrey to get his belongings from the lighthouse.

"Am I under arrest?"

"We have some more questions for you. Officer Matte's waiting for you outside."

The clergyman stammered something and went out, hanging his head.

"Will you come to the harbour with me, Dr. Robidoux?" asked Plogueuil. "The boat's alongside."

The wind had dropped, like a party-goer who passes out on a sofa. Below, they spotted the Coast Guard patrol boat steaming near the jetty.

"My doctor advised me to walk every day. Cholesterol's something like a western: there's the good and the bad."

"Studies have shown that a policeman's life expectancy is two years less than average."

"Why didn't you tell me you'd slept with Charlene?"

François Robidoux stopped short, feigned indignation, and lost his composure. His lips started to quiver. He swore and kicked a stone in the direction of a Labrador retriever.

"Missed," Plogueuil observed. "You've got yourself in a nice mess. Now tell me the truth."

Terrified and on the verge of tears, the young doctor gave him a detailed account of what had happened the night before.

"Is that your story?"

"It's the truth," said François Robidoux. "I didn't kill Charlene Collins. You know that. Why would I do such a thing?"

Robidoux tried every way he knew to break down the policeman's placidity. Plogueuil, with his hands in his overcoat pockets, advanced flat-footed, his eyes downcast to avoid the mud puddles.

"I have enough information to bring you in as a material witness. Did Charlene's father know she was going to meet you?"

"Probably. They were very close."

"Mrs. Patterson too?"

"Yes. The whole island must know."

"Was she the one who gave you those pants?"

"Yes."

"They look a lot better on you than the ones you were wearing this morning. Don't you find it strange that all these people lie during a murder investigation?"

"This is Entry Island."

"A truly distinct society. How long was it between the time that Charlene ran away and the time Father Jeffrey left?"

"Fifteen or twenty minutes."

"Did she mention Randy at all? He was in love with her."

"First I've heard of it. I'm sure she wasn't in love with him."

"Obviously. You're the one she was in love with. Am I right?"

The sergeant stopped in the middle of the road. A

man offered to pick them up in his truck but the sergeant didn't respond.

"I think she loved me."

"Ah!"

They came to the harbour. Randy Aitkens was on the wharf, surrounded by the usual crowd. Margie Stone's oilskin provided a bright note in the grey tableau. Robidoux took a quick look at the policeman. Was he making a fool of himself? Despite his show of indifference, this investigation had come a long way since the day before.

"Old Eva is dying," said François Robidoux. "Timmy Collins isn't doing so well either."

"Mrs. Patterson will take care of them."

"I'm worried about her too. Have you seen her today? She's acting very peculiar."

"She drinks," said the policeman.

"Eva Patton says that she murdered her son."

"Eva's dying. Hasn't got all her wits about her."

"The family treats Mrs. Patterson very strangely."

"She's an outsider. When did Eva tell you that?"

"Yesterday. She may be dying but she still has all her marbles."

"Do you think there's any connection with the murder?"

"It occurred to me."

"We'll have time to go into that at Cap-aux-Meules."

Charlene Collins's coffin had been stowed on the rear deck of the patrol boat. The sailor had cast off the moorings. In the cabin, François Robidoux could make out the silhouettes of Radio-Canada, the priest, and Dr. Pépin.

"I want to stay on the island, Sergeant."

Plogueuil looked at the young doctor.

"Eva Patton is going to die soon. I wouldn't feel right about leaving."

"People have been dying at home on this island for two hundred years. The old lady probably can't tell the difference between you and her rocking chair."

"There's also Timmy Collins. He asked me for supper."

"You're a good-hearted man. You're putting me in a difficult situation."

"Do you have a better prison than this island?"

The sergeant hesitated, then left Robidoux free to do as he wanted.

"I want you to be available. I'll call you tomorrow morning."

"I'll be at the house."

They shook hands. Plogueuil cautiously boarded the launch. They cast off. Margie Stone was trying to get a look at Father Jeffrey, who was lying low in the cabin. The launch aimed its stem towards the waves that were rushing in through the entrance to the harbour. The first sea spray was leaving a dark deposit on the fresh pine of the coffin. While the beams from the light standards started to tremble, the boat headed for Cap-aux-Meules.

Sergeant Plogueuil looked at the wharf. An uneasy feeling came over him. He was blaming it on seasickness until he could distinguish in the midst of the islanders the anguished face of François Robidoux.

"What's wrong?" asked Pépin. "Forget your Gravol?"

The sergeant, usually so affable, told the doctor to shut up, in a tone of voice that made Radio-Canada's almond eyes open very wide.

Chapter 28
The Rabbit's Foot

Randy Aitkens offered to drive François Robidoux to the clinic but the doctor preferred to walk. Randy seemed to want to talk to him but didn't actually say so.

"May I walk with you?" asked Margie Stone.

"If you want," said François.

They left the harbour. The sun sat imposingly on the horizon.

"They'll let Jeffrey go tomorrow," said the woman.

"You seem pretty sure."

"I know him. Why did you stay on the island?"

"One of my patients is dying."

"God! Give me a break! This business is getting to you."

"I've got nothing to do with Charlene Collins's death."

"I've heard things."

"Don't make me laugh."

"Phyllis's house isn't very soundproof. My room's right over the dining room. Sergeant Moreau's a jerk. I'd like to know why he took poor Jeffrey away and left you here. I'm sure he already regrets it."

"You think I killed Charlene?"

"You're too scrupulous. But somebody did it. We're the only outsiders here. People show us what they want us to see. Jeffrey saw Randy's jeep heading for the Collins house last night. I wouldn't be surprised if it was him."

"Why are you telling me this?"

"So you'll open your eyes and do some thinking. When the police are through with Jeffrey you'll be the first suspect."

They arrived at Phyllis's house. Without another word, Margie Stone stepped over Churchill and disappeared.

François Robidoux went past the school, past the houses, then he crossed the fields and came to the foot of Big Hill. He climbed it in the declining light. Distance muffled the rumbling of the trucks. A chilly wind came up again.

When he reached the summit he turned around. In the east, the islands were playing leapfrog in the dusk. Car headlights were scouring the Chemin de la Grave. Closer to him, he could see the entire scene of the tragedy. On his right, the hook of the breakwater and the blue spot formed by the *Melinda D.*, surrounded by the lobster boats. At the foot of the hill, the house where Timmy Collins, with one eye riveted to his telescope, was watching the Coast Guard vessel move away. A little farther, at the clinic, Mrs. Patterson's house and the lighthouse. Finally, on his left, stood Devil's Cape.

Embers were glowing red in the west. His conversations with Plogueuil and Margie Stone had filled him with apprehension. He thought it unlikely that Randy was the murderer. But it had to be someone. Each person would discover after the fact the signs that would have let him unmask the guilty party.

Night was falling. Sitting in the cold grass he tried to recapitulate the facts, but the darkness, the wind, the omnipresence of the sea at his back made him dizzy. For a moment he saw himself at the summit of an enormous peak, the stars near enough to grasp.

He shut his eyes. Death, night, heights—he was

afraid of everything. Gigi Bengale loomed up behind her tragedian's mask. Was it his fears she'd been targeting when she talked about his doctor's world? All his cosy armour—his work, his status as a country notable, the fashionable ideas he plucked from magazines, his bourgeois travels with a knapsack? In her he had hoped to find the violence he lacked. When she'd come with him to the Islands, her daily presence had lightened the demands of seduction. He had wanted to direct the flood of his passion towards increasingly predictable forms of happiness. The principle stayed the same: maintaining a distance. His need for that smile, that body, that craziness was dangerous. Ultimately, needing anything at all was risky.

Gigi Bengale, the Magnificent Tigress, had left him before she was turned into a microwave oven.

The women he'd loved best had been casual acquaintances, girls spotted in airports or met on the street, draped in mystery. For years, he had kept the address of an American he had glimpsed in an Amsterdam hotel. They'd spent ten minutes talking in a cafeteria, between trains.

While Charlene's death was painful, in another sense it suited him. She'd disappeared at the magical moment when her image had become incarnate. From the alchemist's still there had flowed only two perfect hours, in a dark room shaken by the wind. She would always be that creature who was open and without expectations. Tucked away in her death, she would not wither with the passing of time. She didn't threaten him. He could hold on to his round, black memory of her without complications, a rabbit's foot in the back pocket of his life. Their union was sacred and simple. Nothing's easier than being faithful to the dead.

"Charlene. Charlene Collins."

He dropped the words into the night. The wind

scattered their ashes. The memory loomed up, reassur-
ing. He was no longer alone. Margie Stone was right: it
was time he started thinking. He got up and walked
down the hill towards Timmy Collins's house.

It wasn't until the Coast Guard vessel entered the harbour at Cap-aux-Meules that Sergeant Plogueuil realized that some aspects of Charlene Collins's death were liable to stir the imagination of the masses. In spite of the darkness, a crowd of fifty-odd had gathered on the wharf—to say nothing of those who were listening to the radio in the parking lot at Madelipêche. A police car and an ambulance reflected the harsh light of the incandescent lamps. A cameraman was filming the vessel as it came alongside. Beside him, his running-shoes taking in water, a smooth-cheeked reporter was clutching his mike. The local weekly, *Le Fanal*, was on the spot, in the person of its president-founder-editor-treasurer-journalist.

"You're ripe for a press conference, Sergeant," said Officer Matte, combing his moustache at a porthole.

"You promised me a statement," Radio-Canada reproached him. "Now I've lost my scoop."

Under the combined effects of the crossing and the crowd, Father Jeffrey looked like a black-eyed albino.

"You won't load me into a police car in front of TV cameras?"

"Dr. Pépin will drive you to the station," said Plogueuil. "Mario, tell them to meet you there at six. Not another word."

While a delighted Officer Matte was making his TV

appearance, Plogueuil got into a patrol car. The priest, accompanied by the doctor, drove away incognito. Radio-Canada, abandoned once again, joined her colleagues.

Then the coffin was hoisted out of the boat while the crowd looked on in silence. The pine box was covered with sea water.

"She'll keep all right, in brine like that," said a man.

The others told him to be quiet. Officer Matte tore himself away from the microphones and took his place at his superior's side. The back doors of the ambulance were shut and both vehicles took off together, leaving the wharf to the journalists, who, for lack of anything better, fell back on the captain of the Coast Guard vessel.

At the station, Plogueuil interrogated Father Jeffrey again. He couldn't shake off the uncomfortable sensation that had swept over him as he was leaving the island. In spite of François Robidoux's declarations, the capture of Jeffrey, the discovery of Randy Aitkens's nocturnal outing, he still felt that he'd skipped over some key matter. He was holding a handful of strings, with suspects struggling at the ends of them. He wasn't sure they were the right ones.

He released the minister. Around him were officers commenting on the affair, forming groups according to their favourite suspects. He left the others and dictated a lengthy report in which he tried to list the facts chronologically. It was exhausting work. He was getting old. He wasn't used to cases like this. Tomorrow he'd ask for an investigator to be sent from Quebec City.

In front of the journalists, he said as little as possible. Rumours would do their part to put some flesh on the skeleton of this tragedy. A twenty-nine-year-old unmarried woman had been found that morning at the bottom of a cliff on Entry Island. The circumstances surrounding her death remained mysterious. It was premature to advance the possibility of suicide or murder. The police weren't holding any suspects. A post-mortem would be performed on the body that evening in Rimouski. The journalists left, still unsatisfied. Plogueuil got into his Monte Carlo and drove back to his apartment. He ordered in a pizza and collapsed in front of the TV set. Saturday was his tarot night. Not feeling up to dealing with his friends' curiosity, he cancelled. He drank two beers and fell asleep.

He was wakened by the synchronous roaring of Richard Garneau and eighteen thousand fans at the Montreal Forum. He switched off the set. The islanders formed a wall that was too watertight: he needed a stranger's eye.

The phone book listed just one Marie-Anna Boudreau at Havre-Aubert. In a still youthful voice she assured him that she wouldn't be going out before eleven and that she'd be happy to see him.

As he drove through Havre-aux-Basques, Plogueuil could see the lights of the Entry Island wharf on his left. It was mild for this time of year. Every now and then the moon forced apart the clouds and threw a spangled bridge across the bay. The island appeared in silhouette. Puddles left by the tide glistened on the beach. The storm had licked at the dunes, leaving as a calling card nothing but razor clams and the debris of smugglers' lobster traps.

The public housing unit strangely resembled the one where the policeman's mother was sinking into melancholia. The smell of plastic and treated wood, multicoloured doors that opened onto muffled corridors, spick-and-span cubicles where the elderly acclimatized themselves like fragile plants. For these people who had lived all their lives in frame houses insulated with eel grass, there was something dangerous about such modern, tragically airtight structures. Air entered only through the doors and windows—and even then you had to open them a crack. Some of the residents thought that if they were insulated from the salt air that had kept them going all their lives, they'd dry up like codfish in the sun. Most were adapting to their new abodes. Relieved of the headaches of both property and offspring, they found themselves, along with their neighbours from the next township, boarders in a big government-run boarding school. Supervision wasn't strict. As long as they weren't bothered by illness, they had the Saturday night dance, weekday card games, and—if they'd done well on the sale of their houses—Florida in February.

The woman Plogueuil had come to see was in her early sixties, her inquisitive face adorned with the aquiline nose of the Havre Boudreaus. Thick glasses magnified peering eyes adrift in the aftermath of cataracts. She looked like a little girl playing grown-up.

"Come and sit in the living room, Sergeant."

Nurse Boudreau spoke broken French and rolled her r's. Despite the lateness of the hour she had on a dress and make-up and seemed as excited as a teenager going to her first dance.

"You were on your way out, I don't want to. . . . "

"Nothing happens at the Golden Age club before eleven."

The apartment was cluttered with the knick-knacks and photographs the woman hadn't been able to get rid of when she broke up her household. An odour of camphor and lemon drifted in the air. She brought out a bottle of Gordon's gin and two tiny glasses.

"I'm sure you know why I'm here. You used to work at the clinic on Entry, didn't you?"

"That was so long ago. . . . I heard the news this

morning. I thought about you. You probably found the islanders quite close-mouthed?"

"I'm missing some elements. You used to live there. Tell me about the Collinses. Father and daughter."

Nurse Boudreau poured a sip of gin between her mauve lips.

"They always kept to themselves. When Timmy came home after the war he was already an artist, and he didn't care who knew it. He used to spend summers on the island but he was just a spectator. He painted from morning till night. His art was the most important thing for him."

"More than his family?"

"Obviously. For him, his children were pictures that moved. He was interested in what was mysterious about them."

"And his wife?"

"That picture was finished. He'd hung it on the wall."

"It wasn't a great love story?"

"Maybe at first. She was lovely, but too compliant. She had money. He must have appreciated that because it allowed him to paint."

"They had four children, I think?"

"Two boys, two girls. Charlene was the youngest. Collins was particularly fond of her. She was the most rebellious, the most sensitive. When I filled in for Gladys at the clinic, she often used to drop in and see me. She'd pester me all afternoon with questions."

"Didn't her parents worry?"

"Their family life was very loose. The mother would spend all day reading in her bedroom. She knew Charlene was safe with me."

"You know them well."

"We were neighbours. Timmy Collins often used to visit me. Do you know what?"

Nurse Boudreau grabbed the sergeant's arm and leaned towards him.

"He wanted to go to bed with me!"

The sergeant freed himself. The woman took another sip.

"I turned him down. . . . What a fool I was!"

"He liked women?" asked Plogueuil, increasingly uncomfortable.

"He needed to put on his little show. Deep down he was a delinquent. He thought being an artist let him do anything he pleased."

"He wasn't known at the time."

"He acted as if he was. He was convinced he'd succeed. That made him attractive."

The old nurse turned serious and leaned back in her chair.

"This morning when I heard, I saw that all over again."

"Could you imagine a guilty party?"

"Not in the least. For me, Charlene was still the little girl who used to ask me questions. I'm out of touch with the people on the island."

"Did you know Randy Aitkens?"

"Very well. His father ran the general store."

"Did he see much of the Collinses?"

"In the summer, the children used to play in the woods behind the clinic. They built houses and played war. Randy was part of the gang. He was a bashful child. I was surprised when he became mayor."

"Did you know he was in love with Charlene?"

"It doesn't surprise me. Charlene was a little queen, with her court of suitors. They were impressed to hear her talk about Toronto. That's all I know. I stopped going there in the early seventies."

"You started working at Havre-Aubert?"

"Yes. With the trouble she was having with her boy,

Gladys went out less and less. Didn't you know? Robert, her second son, is schizophrenic. He was another of Charlene's suitors. He'd had his first attacks at fourteen. A very unusual case. His father's death didn't help matters. Gladys had to have him committed. She's never got over it."

"It was you she replaced, wasn't it?"

Nurse Boudreau nodded, smiling.

"The islanders were never so glad to see a new nurse. For six months there was a revolution."

"Did you get any news?"

"At the time, Havre-Aubert was the main port in the islands. There was constant traffic of people from Entry on the Chemin de la Grave. My old patients would drop in to say hello when they crossed."

"What about Mrs. Patterson?"

"The revolution finally calmed down."

"After she got married?"

The nurse burst out laughing. She had to wipe her glasses.

"I'm sorry, Sergeant, but that Bill Patterson was such a funny man! It was his only asset. I never understood how he'd got Gladys interested in him. Maybe she was lonely."

"She still seems very lonely. Did you know that old Eva accuses her of killing her son?"

"Eva Patton's always hated Gladys. She tried to talk her son out of marrying her."

"Why?"

"Gladys was a beauty. She had an English accent. She'd visited Europe, her father was a musician. Old Eva thought there was something suspicious about her marrying a lobster fisherman so fast."

"Mrs. Patterson has aged a lot recently."

"I don't know what keeps her there."

Nurse Boudreau pushed the bottle of gin towards

the sergeant's thimble.

"No thanks. Strange, isn't it, that woman leaving England and washing up here on a remote island."

"The continents are islands. We all live on an island. Here, though, we have no illusions."

With her hand Nurse Boudreau drew a circle in space and brought her forefinger down on a flower on the plastic tablecloth. She looked over the top of her glasses and smiled.

Wishing he could ask her why she'd never married, Sergeant Plogueuil put on his coat and left.

Chapter 30
The Lovers and the House of God

At Timmy Collins's house the visitors' trucks had left ruts in the red earth. The arrival of night and the shelter of the hill bathed the house in a strange calm. Snatches of music came from the studio. The doorkeeper-aunt was fiddling with her cards in the light from a small TV set on the table. From a saucepan came an aroma of stew.

François Robidoux walked in. The aunt raised her leaden eyelids.

"Isn't Eva dead?" she asked.

"Not yet."

"Something's not right here. Charlene dies in her twenties and that one takes a century to die. . . . It's like me, all I'm good for is playing solitaire. You ought to get another job, Doctor. You're liable to come down with some disease."

Taken aback, Robidoux stood planted in the middle of the kitchen. The aunt dropped an eight on a nine and pointed to the stairs.

"He's expecting you."

Collins, his white hair barely visible above his leather chair, was absorbed in his music. Light fell on him from a standing lamp, leaving the rest of the studio dim. François recognized the theme from Schubert's *Death and the Maiden*.

"You know it?" Collins asked.

"It's very fitting," said Robidoux.

He'd been expecting to find the painter aged and devastated, but he was only tougher.

"I'm glad you came. You'll stay and eat, won't you? Look."

Collins gestured towards a deck of tarot cards on a table beside him.

"The Lovers and the House of God. Backwards. These are the cards just as Charlene left them before she went to see you."

"See me?"

"Don't play the innocent. I may be paralysed, but I'm not deaf or stupid. Charlene left the house at three a.m. to go and see you. You were her type, she called you as soon as I farted sideways."

"Was it you who told the police?"

"They know? That sergeant's smart enough to have figured it out on his own."

Collins wheeled himself to the top of the stairs and shouted to the aunt to bring up supper.

"I don't understand how you can be so calm," said Robidoux.

"Do you know how many children Mozart had, Doctor? Six, and only two lived more than a year."

He put on the quintet Robidoux had brought him the day before. The music filled the room, light yet charged with private anguish.

"The worst thing about children is having to accept that they can suffer and die for no reason. I started preparing for this moment over twenty years ago, when Charlene could barely walk. Same with the other children. And it was the proper thing to do. My right hand has given me more pain—at least I've still got the left one."

After a long silence, Robidoux asked, "Why did Charlene come back to live on the island?"

"I've always wondered. She said it was her return from Saturn. Ha! ha! She believed all that about the stars and the tarot. She had a good job in Toronto, with a record company. A boyfriend too, some kind of writer. He killed himself when she left, the idiot."

"She never told me about that."

"Are you surprised? She had her secrets."

"It's because of you she came back here."

"Could be. Maybe she needed to mend her childhood before moving on to something else. I wouldn't have let her stay longer. Her death takes that problem off my hands. She'd have had to leave me anyway, sooner or later."

"Were you happy?"

"More than I've ever been with any woman. Ridiculous, isn't it?"

Collins looked at the doctor, helplessness breaking through the proud lucidity of his gaze.

The aunt brought the food upstairs. Collins asked for the bottle of wine he'd been keeping for a special occasion. His loneliness was so great that he took pleasure on this night of mourning in dining with a stranger.

Robidoux looked around the studio. The easels had been folded and stowed in a corner.

"What have you done with your paintings?"

"They're in the junk room. I've finished painting. *Finita la commedia,* as Beethoven said."

"What are you going to do?"

"Don't look at me like that. I'll buy a TV and a satellite dish like everybody else. I've done my share. Painting hasn't given me any pleasure for a long time. I kept at it for Charlene."

"You're still young. Your work's just beginning to be recognized."

"Recognized! Go down in posterity, what a joke! So

they'll put my name in a few books? So the Japanese will buy my pictures? When I started painting I had some ambitions. Timmy Collins, from Entry Island, was going to become a great painter. Being known didn't make me any happier. My glory was built on a misunderstanding. I was admired by snobs who paid more attention to me than to my paintings. To please them I had to plagiarize myself. I turned into a self caricature. I traded my life for a fragment of eternity. When I had it in my hands I realized it was rubbish. Eternity 'Made in Taiwan'. Art's no better than religion: all it does is make us forget that we're going to die, like rats. Do you what I thought about when I saw a painting of mine in the National Gallery?"

"No."

"I remembered that Charlene had learned to read while I was painting. The click happened and in just two weeks she started devouring her little books. When the picture was finished I offered to read her a bedtime story. She said, 'No thanks, I know how to read now.' Today I look at the painting and that's all it says to me."

The aunt, who'd been listening to his speech, slammed the bottle down on the table and left. The sight of the wine subdued Collins's indignation. He peered at the label and, clutching the bottle to him, began uncorking it with his left hand.

"The worst thing about a disability is looking like an idiot when you do the most ordinary things."

"May I?"

"It's all right. I've developed a technique that's quite . . . amazing."

The cork popped. Collins seemed thirsty.

"You're surprised, Doctor? Am I supposed to be sad? You mustn't get too serious about death. That's something you ought to know, in your line of work. Charlene's probably just fine where she is. All this mourning business is hypocritical. People cry more for themselves than for the dead. If they'd just take advantage of what life has to offer, they wouldn't worry so much about other people's deaths. Have you ever noticed, it's the least active, the most inconsequential people who attach the greatest significance to death?"

François Robidoux felt a lump come to his throat. He swallowed some wine.

"If art is just a way to forget about death, why do you paint? Why do you listen to Mozart all day long?"

"Because I'm slightly cracked. Like everybody else. Contradictions, paradoxes—we all feed on those, don't we?"

They ate in silence. The younger man barely drank a single glass of wine. The painter emptied the bottle. Every now and then he seemed completely absent.

"Do your other children know?" asked Robidoux.

"They'll be there tomorrow. All of them. My wife too."

"Charlene was your favourite, wasn't she?"

"She was the kind of child who makes clever remarks that you repeat. She never did what you expected her to do. Tell me, François. . . . What kind of woman was she?"

"What do you mean?"

"What was she like in bed?"

Robidoux clutched his glass, flabbergasted.

"I didn't know her well enough to talk about her. It doesn't concern you."

Collins smiled, on the brink of intoxication.

"I've always thought she was the best of my girls."

The aunt brought tea. The music enveloped them, giving ambiguous contours to their words. The last movement began, very dark. Collins listened.

"Mozart wrote this piece in 1787, during his father's last illness. Listen. The music shifts into major, becomes light and gay. Death is a liberation, don't you think?"

"It's a comforting idea. Few people experience it like that. There are the old people, like Eva. In their case, it may be fatigue more than wisdom."

"You're too serious for your years, Doctor. Are you worrying about the investigation? Don't. You'll soon be beyond suspicion."

"Do you think it was suicide?"

"Goddammit! Do you think a girl would get up from your bed and kill herself?"

"Who did it, then?"

"That's the least of my worries. Maybe it was Borden. Or Father Jeffrey or Randy or any of the maniacs this island's full of. Or maybe it was you, why not?"

"Would you eat with your daughter's murderer?"

"We're all murderers. Through some unconscious or premeditated act, we've all pushed someone into despair. Sometimes their deaths take on the face of disease, but we all kill—so we can go on living. I know I won't hear Charlene's laughter tomorrow. She won't be bringing me news of the island, she won't go back to her tarot cards, she won't sit where you're sitting this evening. There are those real, specific things I'll have to separate myself from, one by one. That bothers me a lot more than the name of her murderer."

Collins sat motionless, huddled in his chair, indifferent to the joyous, exuberant end of the quintet.

François Robidoux stood up, numb and sad, and walked over to the windows. The wind was barely blowing and the island, with all its lights illuminated, was advancing under the lazy progress of the clouds.

"In the meantime, I'm in a nice fix," said Robidoux.

"Don't worry. By tomorrow the guilty party's name

will be known."

"You know who it is?"

The painter, his eyes half closed, nodded.

"I'm surprised you haven't figured it out yet. You were better with the pictures."

"Why haven't you told the police?"

"I'll leave it to the murderer to denounce himself."

"Will he do it?"

"I'm sure of it."

"Tell me who it is," Robidoux pleaded.

"That would rush things. Stop shaking like that. You've got nothing to fear. You have all the elements. Now just exercise your brains a little."

Robidoux sensed that the painter's mind was closing. He wanted to go on talking, to pierce this pretentious sphinx's secret, but he knew he'd get nothing more out of him. He stayed at the window, silent. The moon was shrouded in mist. His reflection stood out more clearly on the glass.

"Wait till it's dark," said Collins. "Doesn't it say in the Bible that it's from the darkness that the light will burst forth?"

François Robidoux laughed harshly. It was time to be going. Collins was a man who made people pay a price for sharing his privacy. For the time being, he remained inert in his chair.

"I'll leave you now, Mr. Collins."

"Don't worry, François. I'm all right—or rather all left. . . . Go to sleep. Mrs. Patterson must be wondering where you are."

"I wanted to tell you. . . . I was very fond of Charlene. I mean . . . I liked her a lot, even though I didn't know her."

The old man gave him a keen, indefinable look. He brought up his left hand and let it fall in a gesture of resignation. His lips were quivering. François Robidoux

raced down the stairs and left the house without bidding the card-player good-night.

Chapter 31
Plogueuil Overdoes It

After leaving Marie-Anna Boudreau, Sergeant Plogueuil turned onto the Chemin de la Grave and drove to the end of the wharf. A road sign pointed out the obvious: the road stopped there. He got out of his car. A rusty trawler was pulling on its moorings. The red and green points of the buoys that marked the entrance to the channel swayed sluggishly before the distant shadow of Entry Island.

The island was round and squat. Seen from Cap-aux-Meules, it stretched out like a gigantic stingray on the water's surface. Like Charlene's death, the island changed depending on your point of view.

Plogueuil walked the length of the wharf. He still felt uneasy. Why had he let Robidoux stay behind? Had he been negligent in leaving the islanders to themselves? Wasn't the murderer still at large?

A big Plymouth drove onto the wharf. Three young guys squeezed into the front seat were imbibing some courage before crossing over to the bars of Cap-aux-Meules. When they recognized the inspector, they hid their bottles of beer between their thighs and quickly turned around.

Plogueuil watched the car drive away. He pictured the teenage Charlene laughing her head off as she sat in the back-seat of a car. The further he got in the investigation, the more convinced he was that the past would provide the answers to his questions.

He went to the Cap-aux-Meules hospital. The emergency ward was quiet. His arrival stirred the nurses' curiosity. Reluctantly, the supervisor showed him to a basement room, where he looked up the slim file on Bill Patterson. It contained a medical note and an autopsy report.

12/04/70

38-year-old patient died suddenly on Entry Island last night. No known illness. Patient's wife, a nurse, claims he got up complaining of a violent headache. He presented with convulsions before falling into a coma. Died fifteen minutes later without regaining consciousness, probably due to cerebral hemorrhage.

Despite my reassurances, Mrs. Patterson insisted on an autopsy.

The autopsy confirmed the presence of a hemorrhage. But even with an autopsy report, Mrs. Patterson hadn't been able to silence her mother-in-law's accusations.

Plogueuil left the hospital and went to the Hôtel des Îles bar. Some friends suggested a card game but he turned them down. He sat at the end of the bar drinking coffee while he studied the list he'd got from Randy Aitkens. In the purple neon light he scribbled initials, arrows, dates.

An hour later he asked for the phone.

Chapter 32
Charlene's Necklace

The salt air calmed François Robidoux. Leaving the Collins house behind him, he made his way to the clinic. The spruce woods formed a black scar on the island's surface. He disappeared into the trees, heart pounding behind his ribs. The woods came to life around him, the treetops rustling in the slight wind, their trunks swaying, under the spell of the music that descended from the stars. He heard crackling sounds in the carpet of pinecones—the rustling of snakes and field mice, the murmur of water trickling between the roots.

His eyes grew accustomed to the dark and he walked on. The spruce trees saturated with water smelled of Christmas. He saw again the Christmas of his childhood, the tree that a man with a funny accent brought in through the kitchen, his mother following with her broom to sweep the needles off the oak floor, while he sat silently in the living room, intoxicated by the scent of the giant tree, dreaming of the dark forests it had been wrenched from. On the right, he saw the treehouse he'd glimpsed that afternoon. He went to the base of the three willows and climbed onto the platform. A threadbare armchair begged to be delivered from the tyranny of those who ruled the place. François Robidoux took a seat. The sea glittered through the high branches.

Timmy Collins knew who had killed his daughter. All day he'd been putting on an act for the police, sure that the murderer would give himself up. The matter would be settled on the island, without the authorities' knowledge. That's the way it had always been. Was it naive of him to think it would be any different? Hadn't he stayed on the island so he'd be there for the outcome of the drama? To untangle the web of suspicions that was tightening around him he'd have to be there. While he was preoccupied with exonerating himself, he still had the impression that he would avenge Charlene by unmasking the killer. Is anything more illusory than revenge? Charlene would have been the first to chortle at the sight of him playing Sherlock Holmes.

"Just use your head." He who revelled in difficult cases was powerless to see clearly the events of the previous night. One conclusion seemed likely: it was not a foul murder. Collins's attitude, the conspiratorial atmosphere that weighed heavily on the island, gave him a hunch about other motives. Some key elements were still buried in memories.

He climbed down, walked through the woods and along the cliff to the lighthouse-keeper's house. It was deserted. An orange ribbon sealed the front door. Father Jeffrey hadn't done the deed. Charlene would have kneed him.

Robidoux knew that all this hanging around was only postponing the moment when he'd go inside and shut himself away for the night. He took the road to the clinic. There was a light on at Mrs. Patterson's. He resisted an urge to drop in. The Tchaikovsky evening had left a bitter aftertaste. Maybe he'd find her in the same state as the night before, drunk and weepy, and filled with that desperate affection that made him bristle.

Back at the clinic he saw the brandy glasses from the previous night. The phone rang. It was Mrs. Patterson, wanting to know about his conversations with Plogueuil and Collins. He answered evasively.

"How was Timmy?"

"Same as ever."

"What's wrong? Don't you trust me any more?"

"I'm not in the mood to talk. I'm tired."

"You overdid it last night. My sister-in-law just called. Eva doesn't have long. I'll come and pick you up."

François Robidoux dashed some cold water on his face. The hiccups of the nurse's old Ford came to him on the wind. Five minutes later they pulled up at Eva Patton's. The old lady was unconscious, her hands cold and blue. At intervals she filled her lungs with air and came up to the surface. The family was taking turns at her bedside. For form's sake, François Robidoux examined her, then he sought refuge in the living room, where Mrs. Patterson was rocking in silence.

Ted Patterson came to get him. The old lady had stopped breathing. Her neck was taut, her jaw gaping, her skin yellowish against the white sheets. He recorded the death, feeling less anxious than he'd feared, then he discreetly left the room.

"I'm out of certificates," said Mrs. Patterson.

"I'll do like Dr. Bailly. I'll send you one by boat. Aren't you going in to see her?"

"I'm not family."

She gave him the suggestion of a smile. Yesterday's events had cut into her legendary energy. Did Eva's death remind her of her husband's?

"Going back to the clinic?" she asked.

"Yes."

"I'll give you a lift."

"I'd rather walk."

News of the death got around. Neighbours arrived and sat in the kitchen. The doctor slipped out. His behaviour in the dying woman's presence comforted him. He strode beneath the stars, full of nervous energy, humming an Irish song.

Back at the clinic, he washed the dishes and brewed some very strong tea. He drank two cups, switched off the lights, and took the teapot up to his bedroom. Once again he smelled the pillows. The cinnamon scent persisted, indestructible, under the smell of room deodorant. He lay down fully dressed.

It was eleven o'clock—another eight hours till daybreak. Painstakingly, he went over what had happened since he'd boarded the *Gertrude-Béatrice*.

Shortly before midnight, Sergeant Plogueuil phoned to ask if everything was all right.

"Why are you calling me at this hour?"

"I'm sorry I left you on the island."

"Do you think I'm in danger?"

"Probably not. Keep your eyes open."

After promising to call him the next day, Robidoux hung up. Now he was overcome by panic. He locked both doors and checked the windows. Wound up by the caffeine, his brain was running in neutral. He went into every room and looked out the windows, opened a book, put it down. He had cramps and diarrhea. He lay in bed on his stomach with the pillow over his head.

After fifteen minutes of this, his equanimity returned. He unlocked the front door, arranged pillows under the covers to look like a sleeping body, then took Charlene's pillow and hid in a corner of the bedroom, where he could keep an eye on the door and the bed.

The room was bathed in the light of limbo. The silence was broken only by the passing of an occasional truck or the rumble of the refrigerator. An hour later he felt sleep creeping up on him. He went over all his trips in his mind, trying to remember every city, every face —like counting sheep.

Finally, around two o'clock, the door opened softly. The stairs creaked. Someone was approaching very cautiously. François Robidoux bit his lip to keep from fainting. After an interminable wait he saw the tall silhouette of Mrs. Patterson. At her neck, Charlene's necklace shone in the moonlight.

Chapter 33
A Swallow-Dive

Mrs. Patterson stood motionless at the foot of the bed and gazed at the supine form. Robidoux was paralysed. The nurse bent down: she'd discovered the hoax.

"François?"

In a reminder of his brief career as a football player, Robidoux braced himself against the wall and charged, head down, in the direction of the black mass. Mrs. Patterson groaned, struck in the side. The two bodies rolled onto the floor. She put up no resistance as he twisted her arm and turned her onto her stomach. She retched, vomited.

François Robidoux looked at the necklace, obsessed.

"So it's you?"

Mrs. Patterson didn't reply. Her cheek was pressed against the floorboards, her eyes were closed, her breathing noisy. Robidoux released her arm and got to his feet.

"Goddamn lunatic!"

He kicked the door shut and resisted an urge to strike the outstretched woman.

"Why did you do that?"

"I don't know. Don't judge me."

"The judges will."

"I'll spare them the trouble."

"What are you doing here?"

"I wanted to watch you sleep before I left."

She was sitting on the floor Indian-fashion, her head down. He went to get a towel and offered it to her.

"Do you want to come with me?" she asked.

"Where?"

"Where you think."

"I have to turn you in to the police."

"Stop playing sheriff! What do you think they'll do with an old fool like me? They'll show me on television and throw me in the asylum. You can save me from that."

As Robidoux looked at the nurse, his anger gave way to pity.

"Why did you kill Charlene? What did she do to you?"

Mrs. Patterson looked up at him. She was smiling strangely.

"I told you I was in love with you."

"You didn't kill her because of me. That's ridiculous."

"Doesn't a woman of my age have the right to love a young man?"

"You're crazy."

She shrugged. He had an acute sense of his own insignificance before this woman soiled with her own vomit. For years now the virtuoso had been playing debutante. She had shown the world only her surface. He thought he could sense a hint of contempt under her unhealthy love.

"You knew I wasn't in love with you," he said.

"Ten years ago I could have done whatever I wanted with you. It's possible to fall in love with somebody who pulls you out of your apathy."

"Thanks."

"You're vain. You want to seduce but you can't bear it if people love you. And if they get tired of running after you, you claim you've been betrayed."

He walked to the window and looked around.

"Don't worry," said Mrs. Patterson. "Nobody knows I'm here. You despise me, don't you?"

"I loathe you."

"Such language! . . . Would Charlene have been all that happy?"

"That wasn't for you to decide."

"I put my trust in God and in chance. And it cost me my mother, my brother, my father—to say nothing of the others."

"What others?" asked Robidoux, thinking of her interned son.

Mrs. Patterson didn't answer. She struggled to her feet.

"Are you coming?" she asked.

Robidoux felt his fear come back. He tried to think.

"It's the best solution," said the woman. "I've left a letter at the house. It will show that you're innocent."

"What if somebody sees us?"

"I'll leave by the front door, you take the back. We'll go through the woods. You should turn on the answering machine."

Leaving his gaudy slicker behind, François went out the back door. Clouds veiled the moon and a faint breeze from the west was caressing the dark hay. In the neighbouring houses not one window was lit up. The nurse left by the front door, went around the clinic, and met up with him at the opening of the path.

"Walk ahead of me," he ordered.

She gave him a look of amusement.

They crossed the woods, then skirted it towards the cliff. They cleared themselves a path through the tall grass, tacking between young spruce trees that whipped at their waists. The hay was crushed.

"Is this the way you came yesterday?" asked

Robidoux.

"Those policemen are useless. They just had to open their eyes."

The roar of the sea grew louder as they came near the promontory. Mrs. Patterson, who was looking straight ahead, tripped on the uneven ground. Robidoux had no clear idea of what would happen next. He felt his heart beating harder and harder in his throat as he came closer to the cliff and felt the sea air on his skin.

They stopped twenty steps from where Borden Welsh had been when he spotted Charlene's body. The sea was roaring. Mrs. Patterson took off her raincoat and spread it over the wet grass. Then she lay down, propped on her elbows, her head thrown back. She looked like an off-season vacationer. Robidoux stood off to the side, shivering in his sweater.

"Are you afraid of me?" asked Mrs. Patterson.

"Yes."

"Come here. I won't hurt you."

He saw Charlene again in the bed at the clinic. He felt like a puppet being manipulated by witches. He stretched out next to the nurse.

"Is your mind made up?"

"I've been thinking about it for a long time."

"Tell me what happened last night."

"I saw you leave the house and go to the harbour. I got dressed and followed you. I lost sight of you. On my way past the church I saw Charlene coming in the opposite direction. I hid and saw her go in the back door of the clinic. Then I waited at the edge of the woods. I knew she'd be back, it was inevitable. After that I saw Father Jeffrey through the office window. Ten minutes later Charlene showed up in the yard. She was running and she had something under her arm. I crossed the woods to wait for her at the end of the path. At first I only wanted to play a trick on her."

"You pushed the joke till you'd killed her?"

"It's so vague in my mind. . . . She stayed in the woods for a while. When she emerged from the path I grabbed her arm. She slapped my face. I slapped her back. Then she called me a slut, a crazy old fool, and I went berserk. I kept hitting her and hitting her till she fell. She screamed and I knocked her out with a stone to shut her up. Then I went on hitting her. I was drunk on the sense that I was doing something irreparable, that I was crossing a barrier, justifying my reputation as a murderer."

"Why Charlene?"

"She'd gone to bed with you."

François Robidoux looked at Mrs. Patterson's ravaged face.

"You're lying."

"Let me take my secret and go. It's all I have left."

"Couldn't you plead temporary insanity? A crime of passion?"

A weak smile lit up the battered face. The sea brightened before their eyes.

"I'd rather die here than in the asylum. I've long outlived my time already."

They fell silent. Mrs. Patterson snuggled up to the doctor.

"Too bad you didn't leave me some room in your life. I didn't ask for much, a visit now and then. I'd have given you advice. You could have pursued your career, married, had children."

"A real mother. But you have your own children."

"People live too many things through their children. After a while it's impossible to make a fresh start."

"It wasn't a mother's love that you needed last night."

"I hadn't made love since Bill died. Except once,

with some poor devil in Saskatoon. He nearly died of fright!"

"In ten years, though, there must have been men interested in you."

"I was Mrs. Patterson, the Entry Island nurse. The perfect widow. Nobody dared to come near me. Except you, but you didn't realize it."

"Why did you take Charlene's necklace?"

"When I realized she was dead I lay down beside her. I wanted to die, to freeze to death right there. Then I told myself that wouldn't bring her back. I loaded her onto my shoulders and brought her here. Before I pushed her off I unfastened the necklace."

"Give it to me."

"You loved her that much?"

"I'd like something to remember her by."

Mrs. Patterson took off the necklace and dropped it into her wide palm. Two devils grimaced at the tips of a silver half-moon.

"It's impossible."

She raised her arm to throw it off the cliff. He grabbed her wrist to stop her.

"You want it that badly? You can have it on one condition: don't mention it to anybody. Hide it and don't say a word, especially not to the sergeant."

Robidoux took back the piece of jewellery.

"Now kiss me."

He hesitated for a fraction of a second. Her breath smelled terrible. Kissing her, he had the absurd impression he was killing her.

"Chicken."

"Aren't you afraid of dying?"

"Today or twenty years from now, what's the difference?"

"Twenty years."

"Twenty years of what? And what if it's better on

the other side?"

"What if there's nothing?"

"That would be perfect. When we look into the void, isn't it blue that we see?"

She kissed him. Her lips were dry and cracked.

She stood up. He had to struggle to keep from holding her back. She advanced to the edge of the cliff. She aligned her feet, the toes barely jutting out over the edge. She bent her knees and propelled herself nimbly into the void. He watched her spread her arms, sketch a swallow-dive. And disappear.

The booming of the waves muffled the sound as Mrs. Patterson's body fell. Behind the clouds, stars were blinking. Lying on his back, François Robidoux was lost in the contemplation of their ambiguous semaphore. As a child, he had spent two weeks every July at an uncle's place near the Richelieu River. One year a boy had drowned. He'd lived half a mile downstream, in a cottage hidden by the trees. The search for his body had gone on for days. The river became an object of suspicion for François and his friends. If they spied even one piece of wood on the surface, they'd get out of the water and race—their bare feet making the bridges tremble—towards terra firma. The oldest boys would tell stories to frighten the others. The parents whispered at the hour when the mosquitoes came out. He would fall asleep late at night and see the body floating underwater. When his cousins were sleeping he would kneel at his bedside. "Please God, don't let me drown, and let them find the little boy before the pike eat his eyes."

When they learned that the body had been found, they went swimming in the pitch-dark, uttering cries of victory. His holidays were already over.

He didn't dare to look at the bottom of the cliff. He was afraid of catching a glimpse of Mrs. Patterson half-dead, floundering among the rocks. He summoned up the strength to stand. The body was tumbling through the breakers like a sweater in a washing machine. It would drift out to sea.

He clutched the necklace in his hand, crammed it into a pocket, and went across the fields to Mrs. Patterson's house. He moved cautiously, shivering with cold, fear, and exhaustion. The fluorescent light on the stove cast a feeble light over the main floor. Not a soul anywhere in the vicinity. He took off his shoes and, with his hand inside the sleeve of his sweater, grabbed the door-handle.

Mrs. Patterson had thought of everything: the door was unlocked. A sheet of paper folded in three lay conspicuously on the kitchen table. Resisting the urge to read it, he went to the living room and rummaged in the bookcase, behind the records, under the cushions, careful not to leave any prints. The entire Patterson family smiled from the wainscoting. Bill Patterson, in his wedding suit, beamed at the side of his wife. Portlier, he posed by his boat with a halibut, marvelling at the surprises life was dropping into his callused hands. Gladys Hadfield appeared, beautiful and young, smiling or serious, brows knitted above eyes like coals. The two boys hung side by side, one tall and muscular, the other scrawny. They were there as babies, then as eight-year-olds, impeccable in front of a photographer's landscape. Then the younger boy as an adolescent, pale and with his hair falling onto his forehead, a slow-burning Rimbaud. Of the older boy, not a trace, except for one bad snapshot that showed him against the light, on a tractor.

Robidoux went up to Mrs. Patterson's bedroom. He slipped on a pair of gloves he'd found in a drawer. He didn't have to look very long. The nurse had left her diary on her bedside table, in an envelope addressed to her son, Thomas. François went downstairs. In the kitchen, he took Charlene's necklace from his pocket, wiped it off carefully, and dropped it on top of the letter. Then he left, locking the door behind him.

He hurried back to the clinic. He repeated the detour along the cliffs and through the woods, and went in the back door. It was almost four o'clock. He burned Mrs. Patterson's scarf in the living-room wood-stove. He washed the bedroom floor. Nothing on the answering machine. It was unlikely that anyone had seen him go out. Should anyone ask, he'd say that Mrs. Patterson had dropped in to pick up her scarf.

He lay down and started reading the diary.

4 April 1959

Nurse Boudreau offered to replace me for a month. "You need a holiday." I hadn't asked her for anything. She seemed to know that I needed to clear my mind a little.

She arrived today, very jaunty in her round glasses. She's a little over thirty. I'm a good head taller, but I feel frail next to her. She's even-tempered, doesn't worry about anything. She worked here for two years, a year at Grande-Entrée. Now she lives at Havre-Aubert. She carts around her suitcase, some books, no man, no children, maybe no illusions either. We had supper together. The words kept pouring from my mouth without stopping, a hemorrhage. She listened, smiling when I told her about meeting Clarence. He was sad that I was leaving.

"I'll be back in a month."

"A month! You don't know how long a month is! Why did you come to see me? So I'd give you absolution?"

He was grouchy. Since Christmas he's been a lot more energetic. He changes his clothes and does his housework every day. He's enlarging his cabin and talks about buying a boat. He never misses a chance to remind me that he's rich and that he has some good land covered with standing timber in Nova Scotia.

"Just one month, Clarence. . . . "

"Goddammit, I could be dead in a month!"

He's in love with me. I encourage him, it's good for his health.

"Do you want anything from Montreal?"

"Get me some ginseng in Chinatown."

"Ginseng?"

"Wilfred Dickson brought some back from Hong Kong. Apparently it's great stuff. A month from now I won't be good for anything."

"Clarence!"

"I told you. You don't know how long a month is. . . . "

I know very well how long a month is. Even two months, or three, or seven. . . .

5 April 1959

I'm at Havre-Aubert, at the Shea sisters' hotel. Tomorrow, weather permitting, the *North Gaspé* will take me to Montreal.

The place is swarming with customers. Travelling salesmen, dignitaries, women and children, all waiting for the first boat of the season. The men play cards and discuss mysterious transactions. They whisper, watch me when I cross the living room. The old ladies have given me a room downstairs, near their own, to protect me from any advances.

Today is Saturday. A beautiful day. A spit of land between the harbour and the bay is lined with stores and sheds, crowded with pickup trucks and children. There must be a hundred, of all ages, pouring out of ten houses after dinner, like spring calves. They hang around between the sheds, stand in the doorways of stores, run across the thin layer of ice that covers the harbour, laugh at the water lapping under their boots. From the shore I yell at them to watch out. They look at me, puzzled. They don't understand a word of my English. I smile at them. They'll be talking about me over supper. Their parents will tell them: "It must be the nurse from Entry Island." I've become a character, the dark virgin they watch as she hikes up her skirt and flounders along the muddy road.

I've travelled across the village. North of the upper road there's a hill they call "Les Demoiselles." I climbed it to look for the wake of the *North Gaspé* in the ice. *Les Demoiselles*. I'm one myself, a maiden lady. I'm on vacation. I leave behind me Miss Hadfield, the Entry Island nurse. I'm in the mood to do something frivolous.

I go back to the hotel and ask the men to teach me how to play poker.

I am the queen of spades.

6 April 1959

The channel hasn't been marked yet. The *North Gaspé* sailed around Entry Island from the north and worked her way into the bay. When they came out of Mass, everybody from Havre-Aubert, Bassin, and Étang-des-Caps gathered on the wharf. Automobiles are lined up all the way to the courthouse. A holiday today. The big white ship, its hull battered by the St. Lawrence River ice, is towing the spring to the foot of Les Demoiselles.

Two hours later I board her. I enjoy having a small suitcase as my sole possession. I'm bundled up warmly and stay on deck while we sail around the island. Winter is reasserting its rights. The air is icy, damp. The boat disappears into a lunar world where the winds come down from Labrador, from glacier to glacier. I catch a glimpse of the lighthouse, the clinic, and, nestled near the harbour, Clarence's shack.

I stay there on deck, in the same position from which I watched Amsterdam disappear into the distance eleven years ago. Back then, I stood on the lower rung of the ship's rail to put myself at my father's height. I remember details of my Atlantic crossing, the ship crammed with immigrants, the long hours on deck watching the grey water churning beneath the steel hull. Every second took me a little farther from Europe, from the little apartment in London, from ruins and rationing. On the other side of this liquid plain was America. Papa was happy. In the evening he'd play with the musicians on board. Sitting quietly at the table, I'd try to make myself invisible. Now and then he would look up from his instrument and smile at me. Was I still enjoying myself? Did I want to go to bed? I reassured him, by blinking my eyes. He announced to all and sundry that he had an amazing daughter. Everyone on the ship doted on me. The ladies offered me cakes, the men wine—which I turned down politely. It was getting late. My father took off his jacket and I'd hum his jazz tunes as I huddled under a coat. *There will never be another you. . . . Isn't it romantic?*

When the party had run its course he'd pick me up and carry me to the cabin. If he'd had too much to drink he'd wake me up then and I'd guide him to our berths, where he would sing to me and tell me about the Indians. The freighter was rolling across the North Atlantic. Where were we going? The berths were narrow. It was a tight squeeze for two.

One night, between songs, a man whispered something in Papa's ear. He gave up his place to a ten-year-old who played some Bach fugues very skilfully. From the corner of his eye the boy watched for people's reaction. Once the first emotion had passed, conversations and laughter resumed while they waited for the next swing tune. The child quite casually began to syncopate the fugue, transforming it into a stylish interlude. Dad watched, fascinated. People were elbowing around us. The child dropped his reserve and sent enticing smiles all around. There were bravos when he finished.

My father and Hans followed one another at the piano. Around midnight, the boy's mother took him out of the crowd to put him to bed. The next day, Papa made her acquaintance. Maria Grünwald was a melancholy, myopic little German woman with stooped shoulders. She spoke softly in a low-pitched voice. Her husband had been killed in the war. Now she was alone with this little demon who kept plying her with questions.

Hans. He took me to his cabin and showed me the silent keyboard on which he practised his scales. He would have shown me something else if our parents hadn't already been so intimate. "So, your mother, your brother, bang, a bombing?" He gave me a shifty look as he tinkled away on his contraption. "Maybe it was your father who launched the rocket," I was thinking to myself. I had enough to worry about without this monster in my life.

We were approaching Halifax. My father and Maria were walking on the deck, wrapped in fog. He was getting a wife, a son—Germans and musicians into the bargain. Germans and English lived in harmony under the benevolent eye of Handel and Beethoven. I was unmoved. I sang off key, I'd never been able to master an instrument. One night when the sea was heavy Papa moved me into the upper berth.

It would be temporary. In Halifax the infatuation would disperse, like the fog. The Germans would disappear and we'd have to find a way to live among the Indians.

I don't remember much about Nova Scotia—the apartment near the harbour, the school where my classmates laughed at my British accent. Papa gave lessons in a college there. And the Indians were far away, on reservations.

Every week I picked up a letter from Saskatchewan at the post office. A brother of Maria's edited a newspaper there. Papa—who hated writing—sent a reply.

Maria made the trip to Halifax by train. I heard whispers, sighs, behind the door. Her hoarse voice grinding the English language travelled as far as my pillow. There was no need for Dad to make any speeches. We were going out west. He no longer talked about Indians. I was a big girl.

Today he's the one waiting for me, above his store, Hadfield and Grünwald. . . . It sounded good. Two years later the offspring of all the leading families in Saskatoon were playing the trombone or the violin. On Sundays he conducted a chamber orchestra. With his Ukrainian and Hungarian friends, he drowned his spleen in scotch when the concert was over.

9 April 1959

Montreal. I rented a room near the station. This morning I went to Chinatown for Clarence. Spring is corrupting the lower part of the city. The melted snow sings along the length of the sidewalks. I stopped bleeding yesterday. I'm ready.

I found the bar I'd caught a glimpse of last summer. I took a table by myself. I asked for wine. It was early. Regulars were twirling their glasses at the bar. In one corner, a dancer and a guitarist were having a row with the tired belligerence of music-hall partners. I ordered more wine. Customers arrived, most of them artistic-looking men in long hair and sweaters who carved the universe into slices in the smoke of their cigarettes.

They looked at me from a corner of their eyes. The show got under way. The girl sang lethargically, her back arched. From the beginning of time, the devil had a revolver pointed at her back. Beside her, the guitarist lost himself in flashes of virtuosity while he peered around the room. The customers watched them inattentively. Applause greeted incomprehensible allusions. The girl arched her back a little more. The monotonous song started up again, punctuated by snatches of conversation, the tinkling of glasses, the creak of the swinging door. A waiter manoeuvred stylishly between the tables, dark-lidded, contemplating murder.

A man approached me. He spoke English. He courted me well enough and I took him up to my room. He was talkative, asked a thousand questions. I just wanted it to be over so we could begin again, more comfortably. He was surprised that I was a virgin, and flattered at the bargain. He thought I was slightly crazy.

I studied his penis. It was shrivelled up, the hairs tangled and sticky. The sperm felt slippery to my finger, it tasted salty. The man looked at me, uncomfortable.

"Want to taste?"

He shook his head. His penis rose, a medieval engine of war. He entered me again. I felt nothing. Someone was talking to me through the grille of a confessional. I waited, curious, for him to come.

I had nothing to say to him. He asked for my address. He was nervous, probably thinking about what he'd tell his wife. After he left I caressed myself, slowly. Pleasure was very near, just behind my anger.

29 April 1959

I've written nothing in this diary since I left Montreal. During my stay out west, I was overcome by apathy. I spent my evenings watching television. Papa and Maria would keep me company until eleven, when Maria would disappear into her room, leaving us in the charge of the Cyclops eye. Dad would get up and pour himself a gin. I'd join him in a couple of drinks, then leave him by himself on the road to drunkenness.

He talked nonstop, wove a skein of memories, plans, suppositions. I bristled at his attempts to get closer to me. In love there's nothing like indifference. Between London and Halifax he had lost the profound conviction that he possessed me wholly, that he was my beloved father for all eternity. Doubt had jammed the delicate mechanism of his nonchalance. Through me, he was trying to find himself—the gifted musician who had given up the piano to devote himself to the oboe, the man who'd loved my mother and had become a doting father, neglecting his art to take his daughter to the park.

I had nothing to do with this comedy. I looked at the snowy screen in the gloom of the living room, sitting next to a ghost whose incarnation I had once adored. Hans burst in, looking like a lecherous Pan. "Hello, sister. . . . " He never missed a chance to wave under my nose, like a rotten egg, our phony kinship. Hello, Hans. Go to hell, Hans. He poured himself a drink and disappeared into the music room. "So long, lovers. . . . " His music came to us, a gibberish of arpeggios and modulations, the elegant convulsion of a poisoned mind. Dad listened for a while, then looked away, sighing. His best pupil had turned out badly. Maria waited for him in the bedroom, unmoving, plagued by insomnia.

"O Canada" signalled the end of programming.

Dad kissed my forehead. We said good-night, holding on in spite of everything to the hope of a more auspicious tomorrow. He went to join his German wife in sleep, each of them with a ghost buried under the rubble. I curled up in my single bed, under the indifferent eye of my teddy bear, who smelled of disinfectant.

I've brought him here. He sits enthroned on my pillow. I washed him with mild soap, scented him with my perfume. He reminds me of Bill.

The island rests in a luminous brightness. The wind has fallen. We're enjoying the respite of spring. Bill stopped by on the pretext of something to fix. He's forgotten how cold I was last month. He hovers like a faithful dog. When I was away the memory of him barely touched me, but now I'm happy to see him again. Under his oafish manner he has flashes of understanding that are overwhelming. He has an instinctive knowledge of certain truths that I, with all my culture, approach like one who is blind.

I'm not in love with him. He knows. He waits, patiently. He takes off my storm windows, brings me herring, entertains me on rainy evenings. The sea always wins out over the rock. "To be in love"—what a strange expression! As if love were a parallel universe, outside of reality, which you could only enter through a hidden door, a flash in the eye of a stranger.

Clarence died while I was away. His niece found him one night in his icy shack. He was sitting on the toilet, frozen, like Rodin's "The Thinker". They had to shift him around the doorway like a piece of furniture to get him out. He was so stiff they had to bury him in the same position, in a cubical coffin, in a square grave. I spread the ginseng over the fresh earth and kept the bottle for wildflowers.

16 May 1959

I waken at dawn to the chugging sound of the boats. They're leaving the harbour for the fishing grounds. They trace a strange ballet around the buoys, small white patches dancing on the crests of the waves, labouring into the wind in the channel's current, moustaches of foam flanking their prow. From the shore you can see the men standing by the gunwales. They haul the traps onto the deck, empty out the lobsters, bait them again. They repeat it all farther away, three hundred times, three hundred traps. It's hard work. They come in after noon, then go out to take up their herring nets.

The days are getting longer. The islanders expend the energy accumulated during winter. There is a frenzy of activities, of chores and errands that leave a scant few hours for sleep. The women are out in the gardens, the old people care for the animals, the children neglect school to prowl around the wharf. I'm useless now. No one has time to be sick. Aches and pains are miraculously healed. The old fishermen forget their twisted knees and head out, galvanized, for a new lobster season, two months of hard labour that will give them over the rest of the year the sense that they're earning their living.

I stay on the sidelines. I've started a vegetable garden. I've turned the soil, drawn lines, and, along with Phyllis, planted potatoes, carrots, turnips in the wavering May sun. With the others I go down to the wharf at two o'clock to admire the catches. Bill is happy. He has bought a still hale and hearty twenty-nine-foot boat equipped with a peculiar siren, and he likes to make it howl at any moment. I hear it in bed in the morning, piercing the flotilla's mingled gasps. During the day its strange cry comes to me through the uproar of the gulls, as if he were trying to wrest me from my daydreams.

28 June 1959
I have a new neighbour, a painter who lives in Toronto and spends the summer here. He arrived yesterday with his family. The wife came to the clinic with her youngest, who has a nasty flu. She has an accent, German or Scandinavian. These city people go to a lot of trouble to look poor. The child was decked out in a cheap dress, open to the winds, that was about as warm as an undershirt. The woman showed an interest in me, to let me know that she isn't prejudiced. Then she turned over her daughter to me so I could clear up the cough that must get on her nerves when she's trying to read her novels.

That's unfair. I'm sure her life isn't easy. The day after they arrived, her husband set up his easel outside. While she was washing the windows and cleaning out the kitchen, he painted, heedless of the children running around him in their bare feet.

I told her the little girl had pneumonia and would need antibiotics. She was astonished. It seemed inconceivable that a child of hers should come down with that kind of illness. She asked me the cost of the medicine and said she'd talk to her husband about it.

That night, worried, I went to see the child. They greeted me warmly, nothing more. It was normal that I'd be concerned about their daughter's health. She had a fever. I gave her a shot without a word. The painter offered me a glass of French wine. There's a case of it in his shed. He's a hard-hearted man, but charming. He asked about my family and my work, and listened attentively. My answers seemed to shed light on some internal debate. I rocked the child in the kitchen while he talked about his own childhood. His wife drank with him, exhausted and very beautiful. Needless to say, when it was time to go I didn't dare bring up the matter of paying for the antibiotics.

The diary ended here, with the appearance of Timothy Collins. Surely she'd gone on writing. There must be other diaries. Why hadn't she left them to her son? François Robidoux tried to imagine the rest: Bill Patterson's patient courtship, their marriage, the arrival of the children, the visits to Saskatoon to Papa-the-musician. Perhaps it was no longer important for Mrs. Patterson to be the witness to her own life.

He switched off the lamp. The *Gertrude-Béatrice* would berth at nine o'clock. Despite his exhaustion he slept badly. All night he struggled in the midst of a gallery of distorted portraits. Through it passed the deeply moving image of a Madonna who had the features of a queen of spades, or of a little girl running through the tall grass. He woke with a start, questioning the half-light: day had not yet broken. He went back to sleep, only to find himself frantically looking for his watch on the bedside table half an hour later. In his confusion, he was placing his salvation in not missing the ferry back to Cap-aux-Meules.

Finally, dawn slipped under the night and tipped it towards the west. The sun came up. The sea ran, slack, to the horizon. He burned the newspaper and walked around the clinic one last time. Like an actor coming on stage, he rediscovered the piquant morning air. He walked to the harbour.

There was a crowd on the wharf. No one had noticed Mrs. Patterson's absence. François Robidoux kept expecting to hear a cry announce the discovery of a body. He stayed off to the side, struggling with a nagging sense that everyone was watching him. The choppy water of the channel sparkled in the sun, which glinted off the white flank of the *Lucy Maud* as she headed for Prince Edward Island. Life was following its course. When he was home again he would be able to put this business into the proper perspective, that of two nights of madness on an island assailed by foul weather.

He boarded the ferry. In the wheelhouse, the first mate was resolutely waiting for him.

"What did you do with the little Anglo? You weren't her type?"

François Robidoux wasn't in a joking mood. He dodged the questions, took a seat, closed his eyes. He felt the boat shudder under the propeller's thrust, then it rolled into the channel. In an hour from now, two at most, he would confront the police.

If the calendar consisted only of Sundays, bachelors would be an endangered species. They'd either commit suicide or decide to imitate ordinary mortals and cope with life in pairs.

Such thoughts were haunting Cyril Moreau, a.k.a. Plogueuil, as sleep deposited him on the shore of the Lord's day. Before him lay the frightening hours that his fellow-citizens would devote to the upkeep of their souls, their families, and their cars. He wished that in this age of technological delirium someone had invented a more radical way of killing time than sitting with Saturday's paper at the Chez Rosaline snack bar.

It was a beautiful day. His neighbour was polishing his car in preparation for eleven o'clock Mass. Memories of the previous day and the sight of his apartment filled his soul with fog. Usually such rancour was dispelled by his first coffee. He was holding a cup when he called Phyllis Dickson. François Robidoux hadn't left the clinic. Mrs. Patterson had been to see him at two a.m. Fifteen minutes later she'd come outside again and disappeared in the direction of the woods.

"Alone?"

"That's what he said."

"Winston didn't follow her?"

"He stayed outside the clinic. You understand, I'd asked him to keep an eye on the doctor. Around four a.m. he saw smoke coming out his chimney."

"Strange time to be lighting a fire. Did the doctor take the boat this morning?"

"He was on the wharf at eight-thirty."

"And Mrs. Patterson?"

"I haven't called her yet. She sleeps in on Sunday."

"Wake her up."

Plogueuil looked at his watch: twenty past ten. The *Gertrude-Béatrice* was at the wharf. He called François Robidoux at home. The doctor was in an excellent mood. Nothing particular had happened.

"Nothing?"

"Mrs. Patterson couldn't sleep. Her mother-in-law's death, most likely. She dropped by the clinic at two a.m."

"Strange."

"She came to pick up a scarf she'd left behind."

"Must be a lot of flu going around."

"I didn't ask her any questions. You know how she is."

The sergeant couldn't get anything more out of him. He asked Robidoux to stay put.

When Plogueuil hung up he felt as if he'd swallowed sulphuric acid.

The snack bar's customers fell silent when he came in. He went to a table, feeling their eyes on the back of his neck. He left his breakfast half-eaten and asked for Rolaids. Walking down the rain-washed sidewalk or driving their American cars in their Sunday best, the parishioners were converging towards High Mass. Their surprise was considerable when they observed the arrival, in mid-sermon, of their pagan of a sergeant. When he sat in the last pew, with his sallow face and rumpled overcoat, he looked like a rubbie who'd come inside to get warm. During the offertory, he forgot to kneel.

Chapter 36
The Black Market

François Robidoux jumped onto the wharf. His Jetta stood waiting for him near some crates of crab. He felt again the mixture of happiness and gloom that always came over him when he was back at home after a long trip. Cap-aux-Meules was dozing. He dropped in at the hospital. The deserted corridors, the smell of antiseptic, the familiar faces filled him with a sense of security. In his office he opened some samples of tranquillizers and swallowed two tablets while he studied himself in the mirror.

At the post office he found a letter from Gigi Bengale, creased and bearing a Burmese stamp. He hadn't heard from her for more than a month—just one phone call on a Sunday morning that had dragged him from the vapours of a serious hangover. He read the letter in his deserted office. It was in her usual style, pages covered with her big backhand scrawl, the date at the lower right. It started abruptly, with no opening salutation, not even a Dear . . .

When I got to Montreal I did my best to hate you. I had to put a few weeks between us. I landed a job and sold the Renault. What do you do with a broken heart and eight thousand dollars? I decided on Asia for the pleasure of telling you from Rangoon that your ghost has vanished.

Burma's a great place to put your own little problems into perspective. It would be good for you. In cafés, in trains, I've had plenty of time to think about us. It wasn't all that simple.

We're strange animals: the flaws we're hardest on in other people are those we can't correct in ourselves. When I reproached you about your fears and your comfort, was I really speaking to you? Was my own intransigence so very brave? I criticized you for living in a doctor's world. Was it any less bourgeois of me to want my freedom? Is a self-image any less despicable than a well-paid job? Isn't it the act of hanging on to something, of wanting something, that is bourgeois?

I left the Islands wrapped in my own integrity. Today I realize that during all those months the only thing I did was haggle over my love. Just like you.

The image came to me yesterday. When I landed in Rangoon, like most passengers I had a bottle of Johnnie Walker and a carton of cigarettes in my suitcase. They bring enough *kyats* on the black market to live comfortably for three days. In Nepal I was advised to wait before I sold them: the farther you are from the airport, the higher the price. Some children came up when I was leaving Customs. They went, "Johnnie Walker, Johnnie Walker," in their little voices. They huddled around me and suggested prices. One was a boy of seven or eight, not too attractive, but with incredible eyes. He stood apart from the others, realizing that his discretion could win me over. He smiled at me. I wanted to sell him my merchandise, but I stuck to my plan and kept going to the taxi.

During the drive into town the driver started making offers. My acquaintances in Nepal had been right: the price kept going up, like the numbers on the meter. Finally, exhausted, I sold the scotch and the cigarettes to the trishaw driver who took me to the hotel. He gave me fifty *kyats* more than I'd been offered outside Customs. I left my bag in my room and went down to the bar. The beer was lukewarm, undrinkable. I was sorry I hadn't reacted to the smile of the little boy at the airport.

That was when I thought of you and this sentence came to me: "We loved each other on the black market." That's why it was so easy for us to break up: we were both waiting for a better deal.

Does that shock you? While we were making love or plans for the future, we were like rug merchants sitting around a table over tea. Our bodies rejoiced but our hearts were doing the bookkeeping. As the guy in *An American Dream* would say, we are two "old souls". We need a young soul to tear us away from ourselves.

Look at me quoting Norman Mailer! That must make you proud. You almost managed to turn me into an intellectual. . . .

Don't worry. This is no Krishnamurti trip. The Burmese don't aspire to nirvana. They want dollars, lots of dollars, to transform the cage in which we go to admire them, shuddering. That's been my strangest discovery on this trip: the Far West is here. We westerners are the dreamers. A hundred years from now people will come to admire our churches and our dams, and we'll offer them our hands.

Be well. I hope you find a young soul who'll let you become a Great Doctor. As for me, I haven't despaired of finding a fountain of youth. Or a repair man. There must be such a thing as a reconditioned soul.

There was nothing restorative about the epistle. An irritated François Robidoux stuffed the envelope in his pocket. Sick at heart, his legs leaden with fatigue, he drove to his house. Freud's welcoming barks sounded almost reproachful. He discovered the remains of breakfast from two days ago, and his room in a mess. He put on some Mozart and got down to some serious cleaning. He felt an acute need for order and clarity. Walking past the spice rack, he sniffed the bottle of cinnamon. He tried to whistle. He was safe and sound. Everything had to be neat and tidy for the policemen's visit.

The sergeant called with a few questions about the preceding night. He seemed to have doubts about the scarf story.

François Robidoux took a shower and got into bed. He was surprised by the effect of the tranquillizers. His fear of prison, his remorse, images of Charlene and of Mrs. Patterson paraded past on a giant screen inside his skull. Never had he felt so exhausted. The sheets were warm. He fell asleep.

He woke up at half past eleven, surprised that he hadn't heard from the police. Had the body drifted out to sea? Had Mrs. Patterson been so alone that her disappearance had gone unnoticed? He had something to eat and went down to the beach with Freud. He walked towards Havre-Aubert. The beach seemed immense, pale as ashes in the autumn sun. Waves were chasing terns with their foamy tongues. Perched on delicate feet, the birds gibed at them, darting away as soon as the waves pulled back to peck in the darkened crescent they'd left on the sand.

He sat down facing Entry Island. He heard voices from the dunes. Plogueuil and Officer Matte, up to their ankles in sand, were walking towards him. While the officer wore his usual smile, his superior was in no joking mood.

Freud started to bark.

"Quiet," ordered his master. "They're friends."

Churchill had renounced his sovereignty over the
Phyllis Hotel. People came and went—policemen, pen-
sioners, and witnesses—amid a chaos reminiscent of
those Sundays in July when the island was overrun
with Madelinots, come here to celebrate the end of the
lobster season. With a tear in her eye, Phyllis saw to
everything, except for feeding him dinner.

François Robidoux, slumped in a living-room chair,
met their suspicions with a good nature born of des-
peration. This peaceful Sunday, going by beneath a
cloudless sky, tested him more severely than the previous two days. On the beach he had felt right away that
the sergeant suspected him. Red as a poppy, his necktie
askew, the officer had paced back and forth, disregard-
ing police rules as he dealt out details on the discovery
of Mrs. Patterson's body. After that, he'd piled on
questions about how François had been spending his
time. At his house, they had carried out a search in
accordance with the rules. Jolicoeur had turned up in
the midst of it, incredulous. Plogueuil had discreetly
greeted his fellow poker-player. Before he was evicted,
Jolicoeur had seen the policemen take prints of his
friend's shoes, seize his laundry, and check out the
cellar and the shed.

In the harbour at Cap-aux-Meules, rumours of a
second murder were already making the rounds. Pépin

was on board the Coast Guard vessel.

"Keep this up, François, and I'll suspect you. Two murders in two days! This time we're sure to make the eleven o'clock news! You know they've asked for a detective from Quebec City?"

The sea, sullen for days now, glittered in the sun. Amateur sailors, beer in hand, were taking advantage of this fine Sunday for one last outing, pulling up to the Coast Guard boat to sniff its secrets. The atmosphere on board was lugubrious. The sergeant, grey-faced, was gazing at a point on the horizon. Officer Matte, flanked by a colleague by the name of Babeu, was nervously combing his moustache. François Robidoux didn't know if he should seem indignant or annoyed.

On the island, Plogueuil had ordered François to stay at his disposal, at Phyllis's place. While the two officers were establishing a security zone around Mrs. Patterson's house, Phyllis Dickson, puffing and sniffing, led the sergeant and Dr. Pépin to the corpse.

"I went to Gladys's at half past ten. The door was shut. I didn't think about it at the time but I did make some phone calls. Nobody had seen her. I called Randy and ran to the cape. The body wasn't there. I had a premonition. I asked them to search the open sea. An hour later they found her."

"Why did you have a premonition?" asked the sergeant.

"She'd been depressed for a while."

"Why was the body taken to Eva Patton's?"

"We were in an awkward situation. Gladys had locked her door and nobody could find the key. I wanted to take her to my place but the Pattersons insisted on keeping her."

"The key wasn't on her?"

"Usually she carried a ring of keys in the pocket of her slacks. There was no sign of it."

They went inside. Lying on a table in the living room, Eva Patton, her nose in the air, seemed torn between two emotions: happiness at seeing her daughter-in-law finally punished for her sins, and disgust at having to give up her own bed. The islanders who came pouring into the house didn't know which corpse to focus on. Briefly leaving the grandmother slumbering in her black dress, they went over to peek at the nurse, whose waterlogged clothes were dripping onto the floor. Then they went to the kitchen, the only haven of life in this funereal house, and in an undertone expressed their views on recent events.

Pépin had unpacked his instruments and test-tubes again. While he'd enjoyed playing coroner the day before, he now felt nothing but gloom. When the unusual repeats itself, it becomes threatening. His examination turned up nothing special—some contusions and signs of drowning. Plogueuil searched her clothing, then he went to join his officers at Mrs. Patterson's place.

He found them smoking in front of the house. A dozen children of all shapes and sizes were playing around the security zone, some of them jumping over the tapes, others setting one foot inside, then yelling and running away.

Plogueuil broke a windowpane and went inside, where he found the letter and the necklace.

"This explains everything," said Officer Matte, who was reading over his shoulder. "Mrs. Patterson led us up the garden path."

"Don't let anyone in. And not a word about any of this."

Plogueuil dropped the necklace into an envelope. He spent the morning on a meticulous investigation. At the clinic he searched every room and inspected the stove. He walked through the woods to the place where the body had been recovered. He returned to Phyllis's house, where he interrogated the principal players from the day before—starting with Winston and Randy Aitkens. He visited Timothy Collins. Finally, he shut himself up in Mrs. Patterson's house for more than an hour.

During all this time, François Robidoux had been at Phyllis's house. He had accepted coffee and cookies, listened unenthusiastically to Margie Stone's plans for settling down, and played chess with Dr. Pépin. The gulf of suspicions was deepening around him. Behind the kindness of those he talked to, he sensed the same uneasy compassion that he felt in the presence of cancer patients. His mind worked furiously to shore up his story. Now he just had to stick to his sworn statement. The letter and the necklace should be enough to get rid of suspicions. The only danger was that someone might have seen him with Mrs. Patterson, between the clinic and Devil's Cape.

François couldn't shake off his fear. One false move and he'd be accused, condemned, his career ruined, his family appalled. How could he, in just three days, have got himself in such a hornets' nest?

At dusk, Plogueuil showed up with his henchmen. Officer Babeu deposited a cardboard box in the living room. The sergeant asked Margie Stone and Winston to leave. Phyllis prepared to follow them.

"Stay. Your presence may be helpful. Before my colleague from Quebec City arrives, we're going to recapitulate the situation."

With his sweating brow, dull complexion, and hunched shoulders, Plogueuil seemed to be emerging from an introduction to the lambada.

"The two deaths occurred twenty-four hours apart. Both victims were women. Their bodies were found in the same place. By a strange coincidence, both called on

Dr. Robidoux in the middle of the night, at the clinic. In fact Dr. Robidoux was the last person to see them alive."

"Why on earth would I want to kill them?"

"Who said you'd killed them, Doctor? I'm only trying to put my thoughts in order. Yesterday afternoon you insisted on staying on the island. Why? Why did you say nothing about your affair with Charlene? I made a mistake when I didn't bring you back to Cap-aux-Meules."

The sergeant paused. Robidoux felt himself flushing under the converging gazes of the policemen and Pépin. Phyllis Dickson kept her gaze lowered.

"This morning Mrs. Patterson's body is found. In her house she left a letter in which she accuses herself of murdering Charlene, and a necklace that Timmy Collins swears was his daughter's. Everything is clear: Mrs. Patterson, stricken with remorse, committed suicide. The only thing is, some details don't quite make sense. First of all, the motive. Why would Mrs. Patterson kill Charlene Collins? In her letter, she pleads insanity. It's a weak argument. She was depressed, slightly wacko, but not enough to attack a neighbour. Second, the key. A minor problem, but an embarrassing one. Why would Mrs. Patterson, contrary to all her habits, leave her house without the key and lock the door behind her? Finally, even more peculiar. . . . "

The sergeant stuck his hand in his pocket and took out Charlene's necklace.

"Have you seen this necklace before, Doctor?"

"I saw it around Charlene's neck on the night of the murder."

"That's when Mrs. Patterson would have taken it from her, isn't it?"

"I don't know. Probably, if it was found at her place."

"Mrs. Patterson had the soul of a collector. What do you think of this, Doctor?"

Like a magician, the policeman took from his pocket a silver necklace identical to the first.

Chapter 38
A Fine Mess

In the fifth grade in school, François Robidoux had been required to take part in a performance of the Passion. Because of how he'd had to sweat over every line, his teacher had thought she could spare him by assigning him the part of Pontius Pilate. Wrapped in a bed-sheet, he'd presided, Olympian, over the trial of his rival, Denis Goyette. At the end he rose, plunged his hands into a bowl of water, and said the words: "I wash my hands of him, do with him what you will."

Then he went back to his seat. As well as the character's spinelessness, he'd had to live with the fear of stumbling over his one and only speech. Only his pride kept him from being demoted to legionnaire. A thousand times he repeated the words, at school and at home in the bathroom. He had a tendency to stammer over "I wash my hands. ... " After a calvary that lasted ten days, before forty indulgent parents, he rose, whiter than his toga, and pronounced the cursed sentence, at a speed that wiped out any dramatic effect. He sat down again, relieved and absolutely certain that he was a terrible actor.

Sergeant Plogueuil stood before him. For want of a bowl of water, he held a silver necklace in each hand. With mouth agape, François Robidoux searched for his words, realizing that surprise was enough to confound him.

"What does that prove?" he got out finally.

"Not a thing," said Plogueuil. "It brings up some questions. Why would Mrs. Patterson have left Charlene's necklace next to her own admission of guilt if she already had one exactly like it in her jewellery box?"

"But the letter's in her writing, isn't it?" Pépin intervened.

"It is, but someone may have encouraged her to write it. That same someone, to be sure of diverting suspicions, left the necklace on the table, not knowing she already had one. The person left, locking the door, even though the key was inside. . . . "

Triumphant, Plogueuil held up the nurse's keys.

"Am I right, Dr. Robidoux?"

"Probably."

"Do you have any ideas about the identity of that person?"

"Not the slightest."

"It's you."

François Robidoux tried to show indignation. He stood up, voiced some protests, waved his arms. In the policemen's eyes (and, even worse, in Dr. Pépin's) he could see that he wasn't getting across. As usual, his acting was unconvincing.

He dropped his arms and started pacing the room. Lying had made him lose the credibility that would have allowed him to cling to his primitive version. He had no choice now but to convince Plogueuil of Mrs. Patterson's guilt.

Head down, he recounted the night's events: Mrs. Patterson's visit, their walk to the cliff, the suicide, his foray into her house, the necklace that he'd left beside the letter, the diary. They listened suspiciously. At one point Officer Matte snickered.

"That's all I have to say," Robidoux concluded.

"Mrs. Patterson killed Charlene Collins. It's there in her own writing. Do you really think she was the type to dictate a murder confession?"

"She was in love with you," said Plogueuil.

Those words, uttered in a gentle voice, overwhelmed the young doctor. He sat down again, shaking his head.

"Besides, there's a flaw in your story," Plogueuil went on. "The motive. Why would Mrs. Patterson kill Charlene Collins?"

"She wouldn't tell me. She said it was her secret."

Phyllis Dickson answered the phone. The new nurse at the clinic wanted to speak to François Robidoux. A man had come in with a cut that needed sutures.

With an irritated gesture, the sergeant gave him permission to tend to the injured man. Distraught, hunched over, François Robidoux went out between the two officers. On his way to the clinic he tried to take advantage of the diversion to think up some new arguments, to devise a plan of action. Briefly, he even considered running away and throwing himself off the cape like Charlene. He didn't think much of that solution.

At the clinic, the young nurse was intrigued by the policemen's presence. A strapping fellow of twenty-five was soaking his hand in an iodine solution. François Robidoux examined him and went to his filing cabinet to get the man's file. He looked at the injured man's face, trying automatically, despite his own problems, to come up with his family name.

"What do I look under? Collins?"

"Patterson."

The nurse thought Dr. Robidoux was drunk. For a good fifteen seconds he stood with his hand in the filing cabinet, gaze fixed on the face of his patient. A moment later he shouted triumphantly and burst into demented laughter. The two policemen approached.

The doctor calmed down right away.

"Don't worry. I just had an idea about something."

He sat down and there was a smile on his lips as he sewed up Thomas Patterson's hand.

François Robidoux finished his work. Officer Matte didn't take his eyes off him. Alone in his clan, Thomas Patterson remained aloof, replying with monosyllables to the doctor's questions.

"This man is Mrs. Patterson's son," Robidoux told the policemen. "I'm sure he could help the investigation."

The officers exchanged a questioning look. Matte asked Thomas Patterson to come back to Phyllis's with them.

"I don't see what good that would do."

"Why did you go into your mother's house? Didn't you see the security cordons?"

"I'm entitled to go into my own house."

"That doesn't matter," Robidoux interrupted. "I assure you, your presence would be very helpful."

The young man, his finger swathed in an impressive bandage, joined the troop. Night had fallen. The wind carried odours of seaweed and wet earth. The headlights of the mayor's jeep, requisitioned for the occasion, threw shadows onto the gables of Phyllis's house.

When they went in, all eyes turned to the newcomer. Phyllis Dickson, white as a sheet, looked as if she was about to faint.

"This is Mrs. Patterson's son," said Officer Matte.

"He's just arrived."

"I've got a couple of questions to ask him," said the sergeant.

"Let me clear up something first," François Robidoux interjected.

He walked over to the table where Plogueuil had put the two necklaces. They were identical, with the same devils grimacing on the same crescent moons.

François turned to the sergeant. His voice was unsteady.

"You're accusing me of killing Charlene and Mrs. Patterson. I don't know what your reasons are. But you're leaving out one detail: the necklaces. Why would Mrs. Patterson and Charlene have the same necklace?"

"I don't know," said Plogueuil. "Lots of islanders were in Hong Kong during the war."

"Thomas, have you ever seen this necklace?"

Young Patterson studied the piece of jewellery. He had never seen his mother wearing it.

"You've never seen this necklace?" Plogueuil insisted.

"That's perfectly normal," Robidoux interrupted. "Thomas left the island years ago. But there's another reason."

"What's that?"

"Mrs. Patterson never wore it. Not in public, at any rate."

"Why?"

"It was a gift from Timothy Collins," said Robidoux.

"Even assuming that's so, why hide it?"

François Robidoux said nothing. He went over to Thomas Patterson. The younger man gave him an unflinching look. The doctor turned around.

"Take a good look at Thomas. He's not a Patterson, he's a Collins."

In the stunned silence, all eyes now focused on

Thomas Patterson's face. As soon as doubt had been introduced, the resemblance appeared dazzling. He was quite obviously the son of Timothy Collins.

"Here's where the two necklaces come from, Sergeant. Collins must have bought two of them in Asia. One he gave to Gladys Hadfield, the other one he kept, no doubt as a sign of some alliance. Recently, he gave Charlene her necklace. The alliance was broken. Two days ago, when Gladys, depressed, saw Charlene wearing the necklace, she killed her. Collins had seduced her, then abandoned her, pregnant. She had married Bill Patterson and buried herself here. Despite everything, when her husband died she hoped to get together with her first love. But Charlene had come back. She'd lost him again."

Thomas Patterson started insulting the doctor. The policemen stood between them. Then the situation became confused. Plogueuil moved towards Robidoux.

"Your story doesn't hold water," he began. "I'm not going to release you because of some vague resemblance."

"You should, though," said Phyllis Dickson. "Every word he said is true."

Thomas

Last night they took away my mother's body, for the autopsy. The sergeant went on the boat with the two doctors. The officers stayed behind to keep an eye on the house. This morning the sergeant came back with a detective from Quebec City. They searched and asked their questions again, with their conspiratorial airs. Phyllis said they'd let the young doctor go.

They've just left now and I'm finally back in the house. They took prints, opened books, studied every article of clothing. They've left me a carcass stripped of its soul, where I'm already a stranger. I wander through the untidy rooms, half child, half man. I take photos, a whole roll of film, before I clean up the house.

I bring down mother's trunk and pack it with the photos, our drawings, anything with a trace of writing on it, her jewellery, even her recipes and Grandpa Patterson's fiddle. I put it next to the relics of his daughter-in-law. I have two faces now, like the moon.

I make a fire in the yard and in it I burn all the rest —clothes, books, trinkets. The crows caw and fly from post to post. People watch me from the neighbouring houses. I know, Bill Patterson's sons have always been peculiar. One's crazy, the other one proud. I have Collins blood in my veins. Artist's blood. I can't recall a single time when he paid me any attention. For him I was one of the little hell-raisers who played war with his children. Yet he knew. Why did I always have a premonition when I looked at him? Through my mother, didn't I hate him?

I wash the sheets and clean the house. The acrid smell of fire comes in the windows. The house is as smooth as a stone. My mother kept everything in her head and in this box of papers. Life is a powerful furnace: when you emerge from it all that remains is slag, images, souvenirs, a joke that's lost after two generations. A white stone on the hill beside the church.

There's a knock at the door. The minister's girl-friend, her cheeks red from the fresh air, comes inside, apologizing. She wants to rent the house for the winter. It doesn't take us long to make the deal. She hangs around for a while. She'd like to talk to me. I show her out. She strides away towards the lighthouse. The sky has turned dark again. The island disappears into a ball of fog.

I've forgotten the attic. I lift up the trap door. Near the opening I find Robert's cradle. Mother was prob-ably going to bring it down and send it to me.

The window in the skylight is cracked open. I go over to close it. There's a painting turned to the wall. Covered in dust, a young woman's body. Above the curve of the shoulder is my mother's face. At the bottom of the picture, almost imperceptible, Collins's signature. Aside from myself, it's all that is left of them.

I bring down the painting and wrap it in two garbage bags. The wind has turned now and it's send-ing the smoke into the house. I set the painting next to the box of papers. I leave the house behind me. I am going to see Timmy Collins.